Advance praise for

DISCO MURDER CITY

"The line between reality and nightmare in DISCO MURDER CITY pulsates with a lurid, neon haze; each song is a siren call to the drugged-up and the damned, and the dancers move to the tempo of their own doom. Bethea's gorgeous, Ginsbergian imagery magnifies the ultraviolence to an exquisite degree, turning up the volume and spectacle until it becomes impossible to look away. Gloria Estefan may have been right: eventually, the rhythm IS going to get you."

— *Lindz McLeod, Author of Sunbathers and Turducken*

"Through a hazy, nightmarish hybrid of gonzo weird-fiction and occult psychedelia, DISCO MURDER CITY delivers unyielding literary diabolism...Loud, violent, and glowing with originality, author Caleb Bethea hits their dancefloor with fiendish panache."

— *Matthew Mitchell, Author of CHAINDEVILS*

"DISCO MURDER CITY's prose flows like a blood-red river, and its blend of urban fantasy, nightmare logic and supernatural slasher horror is a wonder and an absolute delight."

— *Trevor Henderson, Author of Scarewaves, Creature Designer for Tarot*

"In DISCO MURDER CITY, Caleb Bethea drops us into a danceathon dreamworld, leaving us paralyzed by demons with feathered eye sockets, high and hungry for either flesh-flake-sprinkled snails, or maybe just a really nice ham on rye. Bethea's prose sparkles and squirms, guiding us through the squelch of a city possessed; we play detective alongside Netti, uncovering a world of consumption, exploitation, and annihilation. Bethea's skill of deftly lifting up the glistening and gorgeous with a thin blade to reveal the rotting meat below is on full display here, and the kills are sick as hell. Read DISCO MURDER CITY before bed and let it infect your dreams."

— *Emily Costa, Author of Girl on Girl and Until It Feels Right*

DISCO MURDER CITY

Caleb Bethea

A MAUDLIN HOUSE BOOK

MAUDLIN HOUSE

maudlinhouse.net
twitter.com/maudlinhouse

Disco Murder City
Copyright © 2025 by Caleb Bethea
ISBN 979-8-9923773-1-6

For Emily
'til Disco do us part

OPENING KILLS

The sandwich shop is hotter than usual on the night they both die. Gizelle wipes off her makeup at the table, drops the napkin beside her plate. Taran keeps asking her if she wants to try his marbled rye Reuben. She's enjoying the Philly Cheese just fine.

"Are you sure? It looks-" he grimaces. "Revolting."

Gizelle raises the enormous sandwich effortlessly to her face. Steam drifts from the grilled peppers spilling from its sides.

Taran wonders how any food could stay so hot for so long.

She smiles, wondering the same thing.

"How's yours?"

He's eaten half of his Reuben, carefully, in the pattern of the marbling of the bread, following the curves with each successive bite.

Other couples from the Disco walk by the deli, some passing on into the streets and others entering their own order of sandwiches. It's typical of the witching hour, for dates to leave the club and place things in their stomachs, only to return for more dancing at a less liminal hour. Taran and Gizelle discuss whose apartment they should go to after this. The conversation is transactional, starting to be drowned out by the sound of the line at the front counter, men ordering Cubans, women taking the Ham on Rye. Each couple eventually takes a seat as they wait for their order to come out. And each couple is replaced by another one at the line. The deli begins to run out of space and the sandwiches that come out of the kitchen to the tables seem to be more absurdly large than the last time. Even more couples enter the deli. And by the time Gizelle and Taran decide that they'll go back to her place, it's become apparent that they won't be able to squeeze their way out for some time.

Drops of conversations come together in the space between the club-goers and the ceiling of the deli, rippling upward, splashing like a disturbing heel has landed directly in the middle of it all. The noise so loud that Taran and Gizelle lower their faces to the table, heads pressed together so they can hear each other speak. They talk for an hour more. They grow tired. Their words drift into a realm of meaning that, somehow, makes sense of the bodies in motion behind them, the ones they can't see, but feel bustling against them. But they could never understand the extent while fully awake. Soon, two of the bodies surrounding them are their paralysis demons.

They're uncomfortable, these Feather Demons, in the crowd. Torsos body into theirs and the movement sends a stiffness all through their countenance. Feathers begin to fall from their eye sockets. Just one or two at first. Floating side to side in a swing motion around the shuffling of knees and shoes. More come down, straighter now in their fall. Sticking to the floor. Something dark and wet melding them to the tiles. A molted pile of drenched feathers. The demons try to stop it. They hold their hands over their eyes. But the feathers seep out from between their fingers. It's getting worse. Feathers that might as well be bodily fluid.

Something must be done. But their visitees are asleep, paralyzed. The demons hesitate with their hands still tensed against their eyes, getting shoved unintentionally from the crowd around them. Then, they let go. Feathers land with full gravity in fistfuls of clumps on the floor, the table, Taran and Gizelle. They throw their long fingers around the shoulders of their couple and shake them outrageously, ready for them to wake up. To have the couple's conscious mind acknowledge them, send them some-where else where there are less people and pain.

The shaking isn't working. They increase the roughness, slightly. The sound of the crowd in the deli grows unbearable. But, with time, the shaking grows violent, slinging their heads and necks around at all angles, not waking them up, but still shaking them until there's a distinct crack, and then a second one, that pops through the building. A boy at the slicer in the back hears the vertebrae crack off of one another. A man in a fur coat walks by the deli on the sidewalk. He wonders if this is gonna be the shame, the death of these two strangers, that makes him feel again. He has a feeling it won't.

FUR COAT SCREAMS

Netti's an inbetweener. Inside the studio bricked into a mauve-shadowed corner of downtown, the chief animators need a wolf to stand on his tiptoes and disappear around a corner into an alley drifting with fog, veil-like, just enough to obscure the facial features. Netti's one of the bodies, *the* body, drawing each second of the wolf's most fractal movements, forming every moment of the tail slowly disappearing, each variation on a separate sheet, the shadows behind the wolf large and sharply angled. He never talks to the other inbetweeners but they whisper about him. They even mimic his slouch and fix their elbows in the same position as his—attempting to match the hellish pace. He finishes the fangs and he's off to the next sheet. Netti's fast, the fastest on his floor, and he takes breaks frequently. The ones across the hall fucking love him.

On these breaks, he finds himself in the inker's room. It's the next step up, the open space where inbetweeners bring their stacks of only-slightly-differently rendered images. The inkers trace all those sketches on celluloid, and paint it with garish detective purples and dark, dark greens. The colors are supplied at the mixing station. Five men in t-shirts, with biceps too, mix paint and serve it over the counter on repeat to the inkers hard at work. When their own supplies grow low, they grow small as they make their way down a stairwell behind the mixing station, eventually vanishing into the low rumbling sound in the basement. Then, cocky, beautiful, they re-emerge from the stairwell with powders the color of cartoonish panic and intrigue.

It's been a good day. He's finished the wolf's corner moment, and now he's rendering a shot of him disassembling a sink to find the fingerprint of a formless-bodied culprit. He does it quick too. Brings his stack of drawings across the hall, sliding his shoes a little across the tiles, and he drops off the work to his reporting inker with nothing really but a smile. He turns away, throws out his arms. His fur coat screams out his every movement as he shimmies toward the mixing station.

Under industrial rafters, fists beat against the bar to the pace of his approach, drops of villain's green, blinding chartreuse, splashing into the air. The drops leave flecks of colorful stains on their already lightly stained faces. The beat is catchy. They're humming in good rhythm. They sing, with drunkenness, "You're my first. You're my last. You're my everything!"

Netti dances as he approaches, hops in zigzagged patterns, keeping his shoulders still as his hips move snake-like to match his snake skin belt. The inkers continue working, oblivious to the daily routine of an inbetweener and the mixers. He arrives among their gaping eyes with an expected spin on his heel. They clap with mock dignity.

The Mixing Boys ask how he's doing.

"Ever nailing an entrance," Netti takes a bow.

"The inkers are starting to get pissed about it," they flash carnal grins from across the bar.

"Didn't seem like they noticed."

"It's in their body language. The tensed up shoulders," Netti mimes.

"Well, maybe they're jealous."

"Of a tweener?"

"Of the praise received by a tweener," he responds with outlandish formality.

"Are they gonna move you over here, then? If you're so praiseworthy?"

"They said they need me on my current team. They need my speed."

"I've heard talk about the rate at which you can make roguishly furry animals shuffle into alleyways. The Director mentioned something about it in the basement earlier." There is a knowing energy wrapped tight around the Mixing Boys.

"It's a gift heaven only spares to a few, and most snort it all away."

"Wasn't that you though?"

"The old me," Netti spins again. "Before I ran out of drugs for the last two years, two months, and seventeen days."

"Well, that's all good for you, Netti. But you gonna be a stiff if we finally invite you to a Mixing Boys' night on the town?"

He whispers in the tone of a secret, "I love. The town."

"Tonight then. We're going to the Disco."

They leave through the side entrance into an alleyway, only a few turns away from the club. They catcall at stray animals and Netti spins around some more, but the others don't accompany his dancing with their singing. He steps in a puddle in the gutter, something floating past his shoe. He swears and catches up with the others. The lights over the club are purple, violet, and cosmically bright.

There's a sign on the sidewalk that reads something about THIRD THURSDAYS, the message partially obscured by steam rising from a metal grate on the sidewalk. The rusted iron's almost rattling with the force. At the door, two bouncers yawn, both maintaining conversation through bleary looks and off-paced nods that tell the other that, yes, I'm listening-I hear you. Netti and each of the Mixing Boys are admitted with a dutiful slap on the back from the men at the door. He notices that they slap his back in the exact same way as his co-workers, who must go there every other night. This is his first time in a club since the disco came back from the dead.

First, the seats. He trails his friends, canine-like, past the bar crowned by an ASK US ABOUT OUR SPECIAL COCKTAILS sign and around the dance floor to a large booth in the corner, built heavily around a circular table with glitter sealed to its surface by a glassy resin. Sliding into the booth, one of the Mixing Boys flags down a waitress with a python draped over her neck and collar bones. She would have walked right past. Her small notepad is dark and glistening with fresh drink orders already.

They order Netti a purple one, none of the strong stuff at the bottom. More beating on the table. But he doesn't dance to the rhythm they give him this time, blinks sheepishly instead. He is waiting for the waitress to come back so he can look away. One of his favorite songs plays over the dance floor. The python flicks its little tongue.

When she comes back with the purple drink, he eagerly turns his eyes away from the table, past her. Something metallic, green, and vaguely shapeless moves through the floor. It's drifting around the shoulders of dancers clung together in suffocating embraces. Its pace is mild. It is an object covering ground but hardly moving.

It's a Pretty Face demon. With a gorgeous fucking mask. Netti's seen less and less of this level of demonic craftsmanship, mostly just shitty face coverings, clearly assembled in a panic–Pretty Faces being the disquieted type. Thinks to himself, that's a good one. It's moving in a pattern, slipping its way to the fringes of the dance floor, making itself just slightly visible from the tables and the bar, and then disappears deep inside the crowd. As the Mixing Boys talk, Netti keeps his gaze on the crowd. Every time the green mask appears, it's like electricity drifts through his face, pulls his jaw to his cheekbones. He throws in a few quips, most of them self-deprecating, performing an impression of listening. But his attention is on the Pretty Face, and the mask that covers over its rippling lack of features or expression. He eventually states with eyes glazed over that he forgot his lucky pencils at the office, that he needs to make sure none of those other power-hungry inbetweeners take those with them on their way out the door, that artistic types can't be trusted around your personal property. He'll be right back.

Leaving his drink only half-touched, Netti blazes through the crowd, a little nervous he's lost the Pretty Face. The beadwork is unlike anything he's seen with the others, more intricate, complex. It'd be safe to describe it as having a mandala-like quality. Truly hypnotic. And the color too. The deep emerald of the beads is such a creative pop in the flooding of disco lights, like the piece had its future setting in mind during the moment of its creation, that it played against time with each stitch and pull. He's squeezing his way toward the exit when he sees the mask again. It's passing a man in an orange blazer with glitter and chest hair underneath. Netti steps past a bouncer and shoulders by Orange Blazer into the open night air. Looks back and forth, catching sight of the rounding the corner of the block. And, in a few moments, Netti disappears behind the corner.

Orange Blazer is still waiting to get into the club. He has too much bounce to his step, is too friendly with the bouncers. They shrug him toward the crowd and he thanks them for their time tonight. He bounces in with his head swiveling from the floor to the bar, the lights on the ceiling, the full view of the club experience. And, for a moment he's frozen with indecision, so many lights and so many dance partners. The drinks don't look too bad either. He waits in the space between all the other spaces of the club, the bouncers ushering people in with wadded-up dollar bills sliding into their pockets. Orange Blazer has enough for two drinks, one for him and one for someone else. But his nerves are too tight to dance, to meet someone on the floor. He would have to start at the bar, and, to start at the bar, you have to take a piss first. He catches a dark corridor on the other end of the dance floor with a short line of women and men trailing out of it. He makes his way there, even considering a moment of oh, what the hell, I'll join the dancefloor while the line dies down.

He halfheartedly spins and tries to make eye contact with a beautiful woman. She's on drugs and doesn't see him. He keeps walking, taking a shoulder to the face from a much larger man, and he struggles toward the line with a numb face. By the time he swings open the door to the bathroom, men have come and gone, even a few couples, laughing their way back toward the dance floor with disheveled hair and post-fuck red faces. Finally, he's alone in the bathroom.

There's a masked Killer at the sink rinsing his hands. He's tilting his head back-and-forth as if to pop his neck and align his demon vertebrae. His mask is gold, strung through with beads of immaculate complexity, even more celestial than the mask Netti just followed out of the club. But the beads are thick, rough, like snapped branches and bones. His rotating head taking in the ceiling with no eyes. His hands now clean, the Killer reaches toward his knife on the counter. It's a blade made for movement, for dance. In another time, it would've been used in ceremony, in religious sacrifice. But this is the Disco.

The Killer extends his arm, much further than Orange Blazer could've anticipated. A flash across his chest and the man falls to the floor, the door held open by his foot as the chaos grows a little louder outside the bathroom.

The line is never happy when someone passes out in the doorway— another asshole who can't handle his Disco Biscuits. There's a man with a beard, one that's been growing since probably two years earlier. He's had enough of this shit. He grabs the dead body by the foot and drags him into the open, leaving a syrupy smudge of blood on the floor.

Heroically, he rushes to close the wound with both his hands as he looks up at the Killer in the bathroom.

He's cut down at the neck. Part of his trachea separates from his body.

A pair of twins kick the door closed, but the Killer kicks back open—long legs that move in silence. The thud sounds hollow amidst the music. Both are cut down, twin wounds of the torso, ribs jutting out like star signs. Now there's a gap between all the dancers on the floor and the demon with his blade. He tilts his masked face toward the ceiling, just slightly. And walks forward. The crowd parts for him, giving room for his arm and his weapon.

He seems to move slower the further into the floor he gets. The dancers close the gap behind him as soon as he's gone. Safety in numbers, crowds. Panic spread out across them all. The DJ sees what's going on, but she's there to do her job, to keep the music playing and not induce more terror with silence. She's clamoring for seven-inches to make sure there's no moment without music, only alternating rotations of four-on-the-floor beats. The demon's in the center of it all.

Another man with a beard is there too. He's wearing a blue shirt, larger than the bearded man at the bathroom. A frequenter of this club and one of those more familiar with the paralyzing visitations of Pretty Faces, an early experiencer when the demons first came. He wouldn't be surprised if this one followed him from his sleep to his place of work, to dinner, a date's house, to the club. He's seen enough of the masks for them to run together.

Somewhere outside of the club, Netti is safe and unaware, busy stealing something.

The Killer isn't moving. Not even fucking moving. He waits with his blade at his waist, his mask pointed even higher at the ceiling now, rotating from side to side, slowly and off rhythm. The crowd is growing tighter around the two. Standoff seems to be forming. The man with the beard in the blue shirt reaches, testingly, toward the jacket of the demon. He's able to wrap his knuckles slowly around the lapels. He lifts him up to try out the weight of the being. He's heavier than he looks, his slenderness filled with something more dense. But his heels left slightly off the dance floor.

There is purple light radiating underneath the soles of his shoes. The blade is just waiting when a younger club goer reaches for it. Suddenly, a woman behind them feels the blade to her stomach, pulsing out blood and natural acids still attempting to digest their surroundings. Another man beside her goes down with a wound to the shoulder and the knife-point finishes him through his ear. The younger club goer is decapitated, his head vibrant, free in the way it falls to the floor. The man with the beard in a blue shirt loses his legs, several hacks at a time. The femurs only slow him down a little; they make a rich, terrible sound. Then, a breather. There's static under the record needle. The Killer standing with a blade that seems somehow aware of the scene around them.

This is what they do at the Disco.

The dancers form a full circle of emptiness around the Killer, collectively too frightened to run at this point. It would only take one. The chemicals firing against one another in the brain, enough to jolt a person's muscles toward the exit. But no one runs. Light-up tiles flash purple, red, yellow, purple, purple. The Killer's countenance is bathed in purple. It's like the floor itself is malfunctioning in the frozen panic of the moment. The alternating lights are the only thing marking time in the entire space around the Killer.

On the other side of the club, Netti enters with a smile on his face. It's the look of a man who's won something against the odds, a bet, a case, a street fight. A green demon mask hangs slightly out of his fur coat pocket and he tucks it back in before making his way back to the table of the Mixing Boys. He's jaunting, expecting another grand entrance cheered on by his work friends. There's more room in the booth than he remembered.

No one seems to notice he's returned to their table.

His expression is sheepish again, "What the hell is happening, guys?"

"There's been a murder on the floor."

"Fuck's sake," Netti crouches down. "The fuckers got confused again?"

"No, it's not like the others. This one knows what it's doing. Swinging a blade and everything."

"God damn, did they get him yet?"

"Still on the floor," all their heads spinning.

Netti begins deduction, induction, categorizing the drugs that, taken to their extremes, can result in violence with a knife or a machete.

The bass beat leans into the walls all around them, scrambling to make its way out of the building. Netti wonders if people on sidewalks can hear it a block away, even two, or if they're only concerned about the demons that'll paralyze them in their beds tonight.

He, understanding, says, "They're all stuck, aren't they? Frozen out on the floor."

Netti always loved to dance. It started in high school but he was neither the life of the party, or a wallflower. He danced at the same house parties as everyone else. He snorted cocaine off of the same tables as everyone else. They danced on the same rugs, on the same kitchen counters. He loved to move; he still does. So to see a frozen dance floor hurts him on some level. He feels emptiness drifting around his face, like the electricity of withdrawal symptoms whenever he was just twenty-four hours out. He has to do something, so he walks toward the floor, ankles on a swivel, a little style to his heroics, hating this aspect of himself.

Waiting shoulders and emotionless hips, feet that are being stepped on, hands that aren't in the air. He passes them all, they don't move for him. He slides against them. But they don't notice. It's not that long before he's in the center of it all, and he can see the Killer with his knife rotating in hand. Still looking at the ceiling as if to read something that's written in the lights.

Netti stands completely still, notices there's blood all around him. The images of sleep paralysis demons, all of them that must've caused this level of stasis in each of these individuals, conjure themselves into his mind. The floor smells of sweat and iron.

He lifts an open palm toward the crowd on either side of him. He makes eye contact with a few of them, with no confidence or fear really at all. Then he looks at the demon. There's a scratch on the record. It skips against the high note of a tenor, alternating over and over, backed by the pulverizing of a kickdrum. The demon has no sense of rhythm. Not a lack of rhythm so much as it's an absence of feeling what a rhythm could mean at all. A flowing non-musicality to his movements.

Netti, with arms laying flat on both sides, says quietly, with no expectation, "Why aren't you moving?"

The spell of panic is broken. The crowd echoes and writhes against itself, moving in every direction like a pet snake in your palm, but mostly toward the exit that can't fit them all. It's a collective gasp. The kinetic version of paralysis. The Killer cuts them down from behind. They fall forward and backward depending on the position of the others around them. That's how it starts, whole bodies hitting the floor, then the skin of elbows, flecks of hip bones, slices from unanimated lips. The Killer's knife can hardly be seen in the chaos.

Netti has pulled his coat around himself and sweat is splitting from his forehead. He's found a way against the movement toward the exit. He dodges the individuals set in their collective track toward the door. Until finally, he's alone on the floor. On the other side, the Killer hacks at the last fringes of club-goers throwing themselves under the red light by the doors, his body growing small in the mass of theirs, until he's nothing at all, gone. Netti's heart begins to slow, the pace of bodily chemicals causing you to forget your dreams in the first waking moments. He's never been one to remember his dreams. For years, he always had nothing to share at school or work or parties when people brought up the strangest dream they had the other night, laughing at all its absurdities. The only proof that he had dreams at all was the friction marks that dreams left on his body. Bruises that fit the height of the dining room table. Raw skin that felt especially fiery when touching the thick rug laid out upstairs, while he only ever slept downstairs in his room. At the very least, a dreamless form of sleepwalking.

There was one night in high school when he fell asleep at his neighbor Steph's house watching a movie. She left him on the couch and went to her room. Later that night, she woke up to the sight of Netti sleepwalking in her room, anxiously checking the order of the titles on the bookshelf.

She would often joke that she wasn't cool enough for Netti who loved parties, even if no one noticed him there. But Steph was the bookish friend who favored old paperbacks over shining first editions. And she never broke the spine when she opened them up. When they went to school the next day, Netti sensed timidness in her interactions with him, and an animal fear buzzed throughout his body. He was high off a pain killer and wasn't sure what he had confessed, or realized, admitted to himself–to her–before they fell asleep.

But, when Netti finally asked her what the hell was the matter, Steph explained the sleepwalking episode in the tone of someone revealing private news, the kind that's sure to induce shame. But it was a shame that Netti saw in her movements, and he grasped at ideas of what this could mean. And even in the haze of being young and being high, Netti grasped in some way that he might be seeing his own shame on the body of his neighbor.

He can feel it in his own body now. The light clattering sounds of closing up the club bring him back to the crime scene.

The DJ's lowering a steel bar that blocks the door just before sunrise at closing time each morning. There are the lights of sirens drifting through the cracks, but the DJ is doing her job. There's nothing else to do.

He wonders if any of the Mixing Boys are still alive, speculating that their chances are pretty good considering they weren't on the dance floor. The light-up tiles seem weaker when they're not shrouded by side-steps and spin-moves. The DJ is done and she turns toward the bar. She locks eyes with Netti but takes a few moments to register that he's looking at another human. He asks if she could let him out. The DJ nods a small yes and grabs a glass bottle of mineral water from underneath the bar, gives it to Netti for no real reason at all. Maybe it's because people are dead now. Maybe it's because she has an old friend, too, that she feels guilty about.

He's walking in the deep dark before morning. Cars lurch past town on their winding commutes. The neon of restaurants click on all around him. The drive-thru's wrap around parking lots and bus stops fill with bodies. He wonders how it is that he didn't notice the gore on the dance floor on his way out of the club.

The police reach a bottleneck at the door of the club, all focused except for one who's finishing his cigarette, standing to the side, pulling air into ember as he stares off in Netti's direction. That's when he sees the mask hanging out of Netti's pocket. Not minding that the mask is green instead of gold, he elbows an officer to his side, points at the newest addition to Netti's collection.

He's running, only vaguely aware they think his new mask is the same as the Killer's. On aching legs that have been out all night and stolen a mask from a demon. It's a wonder that he can produce any speed at all under the weight of his night. But the police are after him, and he's running..

There's an open alley and he's stepping over some left-out trash cans. He bangs his way down between the walls, the bricks piled several stories above his head. There's a dumpster angled oddly, leaving just enough space for him to squeeze in. His coat fills up all the empty inches as a gang of policemen bounce into the alley with their flashlights flaying the darkness and the fog. They shout about this way and that way. And all but one of them moves on to the next alley. This one has both his flashlight and his nightstick, both held up at eye level, ready to fight a fugitive at any given second. He's checking the trash cans. He's checking the fire escapes. He's getting closer to Netti.

That's when a purple-splattered fist lands on the officer's jaw. The cop reels back, swinging his nightstick. A light spray of blood and spit fly into the air and Netti is surprised to hear the droplets hit the concrete. The struggle becomes blurred and he can't tell who's winning the fight. To him, it seems like they're both being choked to death.

If Netti is going to hit the cop to help the Mixing Boy, he's going to need to prove his innocence sooner rather than later. But he likes the Mixing Boys, and he wants to go to another club with them after work next week. Luckily enough, the night stick has clattered its way away from the altercation.

The sound of gurgling and breathlessness shrieks out of their mouths. He's never done this before, but the weight of the weapon seems just right for this kind of thing.

He brings the stick down on the officer's head. There's a damp cracking sound and it's almost like he can hear eyes rattling around in the aftershock. A couple more wacks. The officer is fast asleep in the alleyway, the fog covering his ankles. Soon, it'll be a full blanket.

"Thanks for the rescue. I wasn't sure y'all made it out of the club."

"Oh, I haven't seen the others. Not too sure if they actually made it or not," the Mixing Boy feels his throat, bruising already.

"You seem okay."

"I stepped on somebody's head," answers the Mixing Boy.

"Attached?"

"There's no way to know. I was in a rush to get out of there."

"Are you hurt?"

Netti tosses the nightstick to the side, notices the thick splat of blood and hair clinging to the wood, "Just wondering if I made things worse. Sometimes it's good just to wait. But I told them all to run. Who the hell knows why they even listen to me. I don't even normally tell people what to do. I'm an inbetweener for God's sake. I'm not even allowed to put colors on the pictures I draw at work."

"Yeah, but you're the best at what you do."

"They keep saying that, but I have a funny way of rewarding it. I'll definitely never be behind the mixing counter."

"Well, I didn't exactly work my way up. My background isn't even in art. Can't draw worth a damn."

"What are you talking about?"

"I got a job because of transferable skill sets. Certain actions tend to slip easily into other spaces."

The Mixing Boy's clambering up a gutter. Netti looks both ways and follows him upward. The city sounds below them start to dull the higher they go and new sounds start to wrap around them. The scratching hisses of the alley replaced by the sliding of furniture and turning of stove knobs. Three floors up, they're breathing lungfuls of wet rust. Netti stares at his knuckles, not even straining, unsure of when his grip became so strong. Above him, the Mixing Boy reaches for a window, opening it with one hand, not even looking in its direction. The motion is silent, done a hundred times before. He's already climbing inside by the time Netti's caught up. A thin cloud of steam and the sound of a hairdryer pour out into the alley. Netti follows inside.

The apartment's living area is lit by one lamp. It makes the couch and floor, the magazines too, all the same shade of cigarette ash orange. The light under the door of the bathroom is a strip of angelic yellow. The hairdryer is strangely deafening. In the hallway, Netti catches a glimpse of the soles of the Mixing Boy's shoes as he exits out the front door. Again, he catches up. They cross the hall into another apartment, this one silent and filled with monolithic plants. There's a Feather Demon rubbing its face against the leaves, angry, looking for relief. Netti thinks of what it would mean to cut one of these stalks and how it would flood the apartment with green waters. He thinks of drowning the demon. But, the flood would separate him from his new friend. He'd spend the rest of the day sloshing around, searching for the Mixing Boy and where he was taking them. But he's already out the window and down a fire escape, climbing across an impossibly thin clothesline to the building across the alley. Netti follows, his boots dangling above the skittering all below him.

The next building is spacious once you crawl into it. The floors are clean, shaking, every inch of them, just slightly. Every tenant has their dryer running a heavy load. It's all the color of the moon. His guide stays close and easy to follow. In this building, Netti's a little faster. He can make it to the other side and not even notice the furniture, the door, or the Pretty Face Demons sitting on the edges of the bed. How they're balancing the same knife between their faces, holding it up with the thick knots that make up their eyeless masks. It must be a kind of game where they come from, playing next to their paralyzed sleepers, two male strippers still zipped up in their pre-game sweat suits. One demon loses the game and the blade falls onto a stripper. His tracksuit bleeds from the elbow, but the paralysis keeps him from stopping the blood. Netti keeps moving. This is the city he lives in.

Even the darkness of the stairwell is accompanied by an ambiance of soft light, rather than an absence of it. The two of them descend each flight in relative unison. And by the time they reach the ground floor, it's almost jarring because of the cadence they developed on the way down. They exit through a lobby rather than a side door or an escape. This lets them out on the sidewalk dotted with the early movements of people on their way to their jobs. Their time on the sidewalk is brief, the next building only a few stops down from the apartment building.

They gather themselves behind a middle-aged man wrestling with the lock of a furniture warehouse. Together, they slip into the door without his noticing, or remotely caring about the presence of intruders. Netti feels at home, the peripheries, darting by an office and then deep into the center of the warehouse, running while hunched over behind a row of wardrobes and China cabinets. And after some turns behind a stack of tables and squeezing through a gauntlet of impossibly packed dining chairs, they reach the end of the warehouse. The Mixing Boy reaches into a tangle of chains and blindly operates some mechanism to open a rolling door, big enough for more than one furniture truck. It's almost humorous, the size of the door. The furniture that had covered their every movement now looks miniature and insignificant in the enormous rectangle of the morning light.

Outside, there's cracked concrete leading toward a brown river with only a rusted rail between the duo and the water. They follow the rail until it opens up onto a river boat with a name emblazoned with block letters across its green sides. Soon, they're among the crowd. On deck with the tourists. The Mixing Boy has been here before, navigated this exact same crowd before, doesn't even flinch when the foghorn blows. The fragments of gleaming binocular light is soon replaced with the dark softness of a descending staircase. They're at the heart of the boat. Footsteps overhead. Machinations turning behind walls.

"What are we doing?" Netti asks, not even out of breath.

"This is the way across the city."

"How are you doing all that? All this?"

"The gutter shuffle?"

"I'm not used to climbing gutters with someone else," Netti answers. "You know—window fiending is usually a lonely gig."

The Mixing Boy laughs with no expression, "It seems like you have a transferable skill set as well."

Netti says nothing.

"Mine is that I could once do surgery on the body. Beautiful surgeries under blinding lights and I could move my scalpel so gracefully. People would come for miles because I knew which paths to cut into their bodies." He looks at Netti, "I miss it sometimes."

"Why are you mixing paint for a cartoon then? It's about a wolf detective."

"I'm a Mixing Boy because my transferable skill is that I can cross the city with the same grace as my old scalpel. You'll see what I mean."

The foghorn blows again. They're close to docking.

They climb the steps and emerge in the many directions of walking legs all around them on deck. At the moment, they are shoulder-to-shoulder with all the other commuters. The ramp to the dock is sharply angled, and a policeman is helping women and children off a large staff at the bottom. Netti is still wearing his fur coat. He would have to bowl through a family and past a pair of honeymooners to get momentum, push himself past the policeman. It wasn't time to attract attention yet, still two miles from the disco where he could begin to prove his innocence.

He pushes his boots hard against the metal grating of the ramp and drops his shoulder into the bodies in front of him. He divides the couple as the woman's hand almost touches the police officer's glove. He's in the air, out of everyone's grasp. He lands further than anticipated and rolls into the asphalt on impact. The fuzz of a walkie-talkie explodes and reinforcements are already on the way. There is the sound of hard-soled shoes slapping after Netti as he runs, wondering where the Mixing Boy is now, if he's back in the belly of the boat, or smoking among the families on vacation, mentioning how he saw a demon his first night here, encouraging them to keep trying if they don't get a visit at first. They'll come, they'll come all right, he assures them.

It's only been what he imagines is a quarter-mile but he's gained considerable ground and believes he's lost the first officer. He can hear the club.

He can hear the scream of the sirens. The heat of sandwich shops drifts heavily over the street and settles in the puddles along the gutter. Tourists catcall him, tug the edge of his coat. A short man with bulging forearms slides what could only be drugs to a woman in a suit on the corner. He must be halfway there.

He starts to notice that the sunset strung above the buildings is tinging blue and neon red. The envoy awaiting his arrival must be the size of the city itself. And when he turns the corner, breaking a line of tourists and journalists with their cameras flashing wildly and in all directions, he sees them all. He expected guns, pistols heavy and pointed straight at him, hammers pulled back. Shotguns with their barrels resting on the door of open cruisers. But there are even swords too, tactical men with bright nervous blades.

The clinking of metal fills the air, shouting from megaphones. He waits on his knees with his hands raised to the sunset, now invisible in the light diffusing all around him.

The light of the interrogation room is warmer than he expected, more orange than white, more inviting than abrasive.

Netti speaks freely, "I don't know how else to explain it other than that. My approach to sobriety is stalking Pretty Face demons and stealing their masks. I have a collection, a new addiction. That's how I explain the habit to myself, anyway. But, if we're being totally honest, there's a deep part of me that doesn't know why the fuck I do it. It works though," his face preforms itself into something more angular and taught, "Just like I bet your partner right there can't explain his thing for your feet. It just works for him."

Then Detective Castra's partner leaves for his desk for the third or fourth time this interview cycle. He takes a swig from a bright, clear bottle, staring away, trying to forget. Resignation hangs around him like a set of wet clothes.

"Mr. Manetti," Castra, unfazed by the in-and-out of her partner, having given up on him and his work a long time ago, redirects, "How do we know that you didn't bring them here? To cure your condition?"

But her face knows this is a ridiculous question, nothing but a Rorschach test.

"Ma'am, with all due respect, how do we know your partner didn't bring you your feet. To cure his condition for loving your feet?"

She shifts paperwork around the desk, laughs a little, and thinks back to a time when she caught him looking at a suspect's ass, the ass of a sex worker wiring money to her disgraced father outside the city. So, Castra stole his Visine—what he used to hide his bloodshot eyes when he got off his shift and went home to his family. And she laughed like she's laughing now, as she pulled out a tab of acid. She'd confiscated it from a man with the entire right side of his head shaved down to the gray skin. Wondered what alley he'd gone off to as she lowered the tab into the eye drops. It was nearing the end of his shift when he coated his eyes, and she poured him a drink to give the drugs plenty of time.

In less than an hour, he was on the sidewalk with his suit crumpled up beside him in the gutter, muttering to himself about how the teeth were too heavy, that they were really bearing down on him this time—the molars especially. His whole body layered with a thin coat of sweat, glowing orange under the sunset.

She gathers herself with the trappings of professionalism, and looks Netti in the eyes, "Do you have any experience with the occult?"

"Ouija boards, yes. Astrology, not much. I did a Tarot reading once—not productive; the death card, in fact. But the disco queen performing the reading told me it didn't mean what I was afraid of. But, if I was afraid, it was the right kind of fear, that I could leannnnn into it. She had the longest blood purple nails. But I'm not sure whether or not that falls into the category. How are you defining the occult?"

"Well, was the card reversed or upright?"

"Said she didn't concert herself with those categories."

Castra lets out an expectant sigh, "Anything to do with the supernatural or paranormal… Let's define it as that," her face concentrates, reflects on the assorted piles of academic degrees and professional training she's collected through the years–all of them earned and accomplished with a great deal of skepticism behind the intense brown of her eyes, "But with a dark streak to it. And you would have had to do something intentional to make it happen, or to interact with it in some way–maybe some art and sex appeal thrown in. Let's call that the occult."

Netti smiles impossibly wide, "That was amazing. A definition. An answer! Most of the time, a detective won't just get to an answer. There has to be a fucking story to it. It's like this miasma of… narrative suffering. All these plots and twists and goddamned anecdotes are screaming to break out from under the skin. And it's heartbreaking because detectives do it because the cities they investigate do it. They can't fucking help it. What else is there to do but ooze and bleed stories from your mouths when even the sandwich shops have their own unique murders and demons. But…" Netti clears his throat, "Not you. You've got an answer for me, tonight, at least. And to answer your question, I'd love to say that I've never been involved in the occult. But, there was a time when I was a teenager, an experience with a Ouija board.

I was at my best friend's house. My neighbor, Steph. May have even mentioned her earlier. Spent the night there all the time. My father was a piece of shit and mom was a detective, actually. So she worked the late hours just like you. So, I was always at Steph's house and we were always into some shit. And that night, we found a pile of dead flies in her room.

I'm not even fucking with you; it was disgusting, just a small pile of dead flies on the window sill. So, we were being dumbasses and flipping them around and shoving them in each other's faces. But that got boring, so we started stringing together theories on how they got there, who piled them up like that. So, of course, all our theories were pretty occult. That there might be a presence out there killing small lives.

There's no motivation behind a crime like that. Which would have made it difficult for my mom, and I don't blame her because it was her job to make collages out of motivations and dirty little violences. But, I'm not like my mom, so I think it set me up for the Ouija experiment in a unique way.

So we gathered up the flies and mashed them across the board with the planchette. We sat with our knees together, moving it across fly guts until the letters were covered up and then uncovered again. You could hear the innards sliding across the wood. Little wings and legs sticking up at the ceiling. And we didn't want to ask any of those inductive reasoning questions. Because those have a completely different set of logic than the suspects we were working with. Asking the who, what, when, how, or something wouldn't get us anywhere. Because, in the end, there's nowhere to go. So, you just ask what you want.

'What's wrong with an insect?
Is it the sound of flight?
Have you always been here?
What about the flies?
Did you come before them?
Did you bring them here?
How many have died?
Was it your fault or ours?
Are you buried here?
Are you buried?

Are you in the attic and the flies are below you?

How many have died?

If it's your fault, would you please tell us?'

And at the end of it, I was streaked with something thin. And warm. I'd gotten really into it, and rubbed the planchette in all directions over my skin and my body. Tracked the questions and fly guts across me. Steph thought it was part of the ritual, and she left me to it.

Castra puts her hand on Netti's knee. Her face has an expression of understanding, the kind people make when someone at a party tries to describe the strangest dream they had the other night but can't remember. She begins speaking, but not in the voice of a detective. The voice of a father, a mother, a neighbor who notices you haven't been sleeping because your light upstairs, your small square of the world, has been glowing through a window out against the night.

"Netti, this is going to be hard. There will be moments you'll feel like your insides want nothing more than to cut through the skin that's holding them together. But, I think you're going to survive this city. I think we both will, and we're going to work together."

Even then, there was something distant in her voice that knew she herself was not telling the truth.

But, he doesn't hear her. He's listening for whatever killed the flies.

A DISCO BABY LIKE ME

The crowd's getting out of hand tonight. The sexual tension hasn't been this thick since before the demons. Netti laughs as he follows his latest gin-glassed acquaintances into a purple-lit back room. The banter's already revealed that they're from a local ad agency. The part of Netti that always loved detectives always had a soft spot for marketers, the cuff links and the way they move their arms during a pitch for the next quarterly project. It's sexy. This team was no different, the way they crossed their legs at the ankles with their timelessly patterned socks.

He stands, drinklessly straightening his fur coat, as the off-clock group sits in a half-circle booth facing him.

"So, do you have any clients that a disco baby like me might have heard of?"

A few of them shuffle their knees, look to one that's wearing a vest.

The Vest swallows an ice cube whole and clears his throat, "Well, we're a startup but have worked our asses off to have a good portfolio. We've got a few pots on a few burners, but our client we're probably most excited about at the moment is the city itself."

"Wow. Congrats on that," he looks around for something to raise for a toast. He grabs an empty from a cocktail table and raises it in the direction of the Vest. "To the city, and telling its story!"

They elbow each other with this-is-our-guy enthusiasm, smiling, their teeth like white voids.

"As much as we love the city, and we want what's best for it," the Vest continues, "the whole demon onslaught has actually been a pretty positive thing for our business. Because like a lot of the other businesses here, some of the more established agencies—who, just between all of us in this room, had gotten a little too monolithic, even stagnant, for years before the demons came—have left the city for safer locations. And, to be frank, that's not us. It's not what we're built on, and it's not what we're interested in long term. If there's not even just a little bit of risk to it, we probably don't have it on the calendar. And nothing against those agencies. You have to do what you have to do, but their approach just isn't for us at the end of the day. But, that's just a little bit about us. That's who we are and a little bit of the context behind why we're happy with how we're positioned in the current moment. And we couldn't be happier to be doing what we do, even stuff like this like after we clock out the end of the day, blow off steam, meet cool new people like yourself. Which is why I'm saying all this because I want to hear a little bit more about you. So, tell me a little bit about yourself. Are you from the city? Have you always lived here? Big disco fan, obviously–I see you with your makeup and…"

"Helps with the scars," Netti points to the lined texture beneath his foundation.

"Yeah, well. Just all of this. Yeah, just tell me, tell us about yourself."

"Yeah, well that's awesome. A lot to say here. But, yeah I grew up here in the city not too far away, just a few blocks west of here. My dad wasn't around and my mom was a detective so that made for an interesting upbringing. Keenly aware of all the crime that went on here in the 70s. But I also had plenty of freedom to get into plenty of the bullshit myself. So I woke up in all kinds of rooms on all kinds of blocks in this city, not knowing how I got there. And what would've been cliche, would be if my detective mom was always coming around and bailing me out. But that wasn't the case at all. The tough love type. Or, she was too busy with work. Either way, I was finding my own way home."

"Well—"

"If you—"

"Oh."

"Sorry, didn't mean to cut you off there."

"Go ahead."

"Okay, so I was just going to ask, where did all this leave you? You had a strong mother, a detective, no less. My god, it's times like these when you really need one. And you were—I'm assuming you could make the argument that you were—becoming a strong young person. So, what are you up to now?"

"Wildly enough, I'm actually an inbetweener for an animation studio."

"No. Kidding."

"Yeah, so I'm one of the boys. Or, one of the guys. Who makes the characters move. The higher-up artists hand us a stack of images, and we copy them with slight alterations, over and over, then make the movement happen. It's old school, not entirely sure how or why the network approved, something about strange times, but I enjoy it. I'm fast at it." Something registers across Netti's face like a new electricity or chemical is moving the muscles behind his expressions. In an instant, he's bright, "Actually—I don't often point this out, especially to strangers, but I've got a feeling we're soon to be friends—but I'm the fastest one on the floor. The Mixing Boys love it."

One of the marketers whispers to another.

Netti continues, "But, I'm also consulting on a case–"

A sly recognition comes over the Vest's face, interrupting Netti, "And we love the Mixing Boys!"

They all laugh, a cornea-thin veil of confusion covers Netti's expression.

The Vest decides he'll be the one to make order of the raucous, "Yeah, I think your boys have done some favors for this crew after hours," he laughs with a practiced cadence. "I've got nothing against them. I'm sure they're a great bunch. Creative types like yourself always are!"

"Well, I'm proud to say that I've been clean for --.

"No. Kidding. Is that, is that something you're comfortable talking more about. I mean, I'm genuinely interested but if you need to tell me to shut up, that is more than okay by me."

"No, no. It's fine. I think the best way to explain it is with my name. Netti's short for Manetti. And the original Manetti was a math guy and a real esoteric type too. One of his things was measuring the opening of hell. Precisely too. Four hundred and fifty miles around the top. So, anyways I tried to measure hell in cocaine lines. Not the most efficient method but it was the most effective when it's all said and done."

"But now you're an artist," one of the marketers on at the end of the bench hooks into the conversation, "That's amazing. I'm an artist too, so I can relate on that level. Not saying that I can relate to every aspect of it, but doing something with your creativity, I love that. And, to be honest, that's my favorite kind of story to tell when we're doing our work. Just meeting people here in the city and showing everyone what's true about them."

The Vest swoops back in, "And if I could add to the great stuff he's already–"

"No, that sounds great. I love telling stories too," Netti interrupts, "I'm a bit of a story whore, actually. Even my day job–I'm drawing thousands of variations of this same wolf. Just infinite portrayals of him peeking into shadows and spying over rooftops. Since my mom was a detective, she was always answering questions by telling stories. I mean, you've been to the theater or flipped on the TV at home. Can't answer a single question straight, just some story. So when–"

"Fun stories or was it life stories?"

"It was both, mostly life stories, stuff she brought home from work, procedures."

"Oh, you have to tell me about that shit."

"Yeah, so it was a lot of yellow tape and flashlights. And some griping about paperwork, and you wouldn't believe how low the salary was back then. But sometimes, she would just go on about big-picture stuff. Almost philosophical. For example, toward the end of her career, she started to develop this theory that individuals couldn't be guilty of a crime. So, you can imagine her superiors weren't thrilled when she wanted to do away with the concept of suspects and replace it with categories. Her thought was that an act as sticky as murder can't be cleaned off until there's just one culprit with something like one to three motivations. I can't remember all the factors she listed—emotional intelligence, workplace resilience, popular culture influences—but she was clear the actual number of factors was infinite. There are essentially so many hands in the final push that make someone commit murder that it's really kind of arbitrary as to which hand is actually holding the knife. Suspects just don't make sense. It's cocky to say who killed who. I mean it's especially cocky to say why that person offed someone.

But, on the other hand, there's a deep human need for justice, especially the punitive kind. And there's a practical element of what to do with a killer.

So she told her boss about a case when the owner and cook behind a bagel shop was being smothered by the IRS. Accountants were in and out of the shop all day. And the bell would ring every damn time they walked in. The poor guy used to love the sound of the bell! Hungry customers. But these people had a different kind of hunger. Nothing whole-grain about it, they wanted a CLOSED sign to hang all flaccid from his door. So they made piles of paperwork, tall beige stacks positioned like little menaces around the bagel shop. It was a complete and total takeover.

My mom said the chef was changing before the eyes of his regulars. His mustache used to be perfect, and he'd let it grow moss-like over his mouth and down his chin. The bagels didn't go unscathed either. Pretty soon, he was serving breakfast stale, stone circles with poppy seeds on top, cream cheese squeezed in the middle. It was a toss-up on what would close him down first, the encroaching audits or the complete absence of customers. People who knew him said he'd gotten testy, not himself, and prone to rage. And the worst part was that you could always hear the auditors cackling outside of the shop, smothering smoked-up cigarettes between their loafers and the concrete. Poor bastard had to walk through a pack of them every time he closed up for the night.

Awful stuff, any man would have snapped in his situation. But, they got to him first. Pinned him in the kitchen one night and cut him out of his skin. Now, that's not the best example because it was an instance of group violence, rather than individual. But the point still shines through, that it was a category of people—accountant-types—who were guilty of the murder. So, in that sense, maybe the story actually illustrates the theory perfectly. So it's this category that needs to be taken into consideration when societal changes are up for grabs. And the idea is that it'll decrease the number of killings over time. So that was her big contribution to the field. Of course, it wasn't received well. But, it's one of my goals to sort of continue her ideas and make sure they stay alive, and not just stay alive, but make a real difference too. I know they will; it's just a matter of proving the results."

"Results? How are you going to prove those?" the one who seemed to be second in command asked.

"Ah, I don't like to mention this out front but I do detective work on the side."

The marketers punched each other's shoulders, their next city campaign coming to life in full discotheque colors.

"Well… go on, you fascinating bastard! Tell us about your side hustle!"

The Vest cuts in, "Firstly – sorry, guys; I just want to put all our cards on the table here – you could probably put the pieces together here, especially considering the bombshell you just dropped on us, but I can speak for my whole team here that we would love nothing more than to share your story through our connections in the media. So, I'll shut up now because I want to hear what you have to say about it, but I just wanted you to know upfront that we're interested in boosting this story in a big way. So, I'm not sure if that changes anything you'd normally share in the privacy of a back room in the club. Just throwing that out there in full disclosure. And, of course, you could tell us to shut the fuck up and walk out of here to protect the privacy of your work. Obviously, we wouldn't hold that against you at all. So just say the word, man."

"No, no. It's fine. Happy to talk about my work. The hurdle really is completely internal. Sometimes I feel like a fraud calling myself a detective, but there's an argument to be made that there's no one thing that a detective is; I guess you could say that the detective is just like the suspect in that you can't boil it down to an individual. It's back to the category again. It's all categories.

So, to answer your question, here's what I'm doing with these theories in my work.

Like everyone else like us, I've been going to the disco. Obviously, the demons can show up anywhere after they get through in your sleep paralysis, but there's something different about the way they stick around when people are on the dance floor. Anywhere else, your bus stop, the Friday night dinner spot, definitely your bedroom, it's like they're some kind of super leech, bred for clinging onto other organisms—millions and millions of years learning how to really get a hold of other life forms. But, at the disco, it's almost romantic. Their presence is easy enough to swallow and you might even look over your shoulder just to check that they're there in the corner observing, but not in a fearful way. Like checking to see if the moon's still there. You know it will be, but you catch yourself looking. It's intoxicating. The way the colored lights make sense of how they move. No other light can do that. Feathers are, of course, wild to watch. I've started considering it good luck if I find any feathers on the sidewalk these days. Could be disease-ridden pigeon's feathers for all I know, but I will pocket it real quickly when everyone is preoccupied with their next destination. But, the Pretty Faces, they're my true love. The masks that they create. The designs are so obviously from another plane that it's nauseating when you really look at them. You can't take your eyes off them. So you get sick, and then even more sick, and just when everything's about to explode out of your face, a really soft electricity warms its way down your neck. You're stable again, calm. And the pattern of the mask makes perfect sense. That's when I'm sure to follow that demon out the exit.

If I do it right, I can sneak into an apartment after the demon and before the person. And it's hard to describe what happens in there, so I usually just tell people what it feels like to steal a mask from a Pretty Face.

Well, you're a bunch of artists; you'll understand this. It's like the euphoria of having a creative breakthrough. Like, when I'm at work drawing a wolf that's supposed to walk this way, but you realize he should actually be leaping instead. That almost panicked feeling of warmth that hits you. That you have to get fucking moving. But, at the same time, there's a stillness to it. Like everything is all one piece. Like everything is the mask itself.

So, I put everything in my pocket, and I take the subway back to my apartment. That's where sometimes—but not all the time—I actually put the mask on. I look at the city from my window and through whatever eyeholes have been cut out of the mask with demon knives."

It's the first time in some time that Netti is paralyzed. Just like mosquitoes suck blood from some, and not from others, Netti experiences very little in the way of visiting demons. And it happens to him enough that this is no surprise, but he is far from used to it. The way his veins orchestrate movements through his body even when his muscles can't move his limbs the way his nervous system decides to keep on breathing, even when he is wretched with panic.

Testing, he moves his eyes from the ceiling to a wall and then to the other side of the room. Full range of motion. Then turns his gaze across his headboard, fearing hands and fingers might be running their way down. Then, he peers over his cheekbones, wondering why he's sitting at the foot of his bed. Empty.

He looks to hook on the wall, his engine for a coat hanging all the way to the floorboards. No, there was no demon to be seen. Only paralysis. He grows nauseous, as nauseous as he is hot. Sweating as he hears its voice for the first time. A Whisper Teeth's voice.

"You wouldn't believe what I just saw. The same motel I visit once a week, in the same room too. There is a hooker with a genuine capacity to do harm. So I've been waiting, for someone not to pay, or go too far, or refuse to leave the room and brave whatever else the winter breeze is swirling around them. But it was none of those things. It was much smaller, or at least I thought it was much smaller. A man showed her a picture of his family. Wife. Kids. Three purebred dogs, all identical. Anyway, by the time it was over, half of his face was gone. An ice bucket of all things, an effective bludgeon when called on. I'm going to visit that man after you.

So we can get to it now. Thank you for having me in your room. Thank you for listening. The last time I did this, I remember feeling as if you could hear me. Really hear me in a way that the others can't. I feel like I can be myself around you, Netti. You make me feel like I don't have to hide the way I hurt people. The way I want to hurt you. And I bet you want to do the same with me. I wouldn't mind. I wish I had a skin so you could split it.

I wanna show you all the bones in my spine. Need to be surprised by how many I can fit inside of me, if only I had a skeleton. What are you gonna do for me? What are you gonna do to get me my skin. I think I've earned it.

Did you open yourself up? Would you give me any of your own skin, of your own insides, a handful of your spine? Oh god what I can do with just three of your vertebrae. Come on, let's try something."

INTERLUDE – OYSTER BRAINS, CARAPACE LUNGS!

The shadow is terrible. He moves languidly against the wall at the back of the club, waving his arms tentacle-like. Laughing, still sober. They'd done it again, bought him a 40 for each hand, and taped it to the right and the left. The only way to free your hands is to finish the 40s. He's done this before, his cheekbones swelling up against his eyes with a smile. But for him, it isn't finishing the bottles. He's been doing that sort of thing since he was 14 years old. And it isn't the secondary question either. What to do when you have to take a piss? He's at the Disco. Plenty of hands to unzip his pants so he can waddle into an alleyway outside. No, for him, it's just the feeling of being stuck. The tape feeling organic around his knuckles and wrists, pulling the glass into his arm and sealing it all into one piece.

He appreciates the separation of things. One thing begins and another ends. Where that thing ends, another starts to take its form. He understands that life necessitates the blurring of these lines. But he relishes in the utility of dividing the objects of his attention. He cut his money into neat decisions according to his budget. His commute is just as regimented as his shift schedule. His meals are just as reliable, the same grocery list every month.

The last time he agreed to something like this, he vomited at the edge of the dance floor. He was crouched down with his useless hands slung behind him like an ape dragging its knuckles, perfectly still, hurling acid and burger onto the purple-lit floor. In the hurling, he felt like a grim part of it all. Swallowed up and vomited out of himself, emerging from between the tiles.

In that moment he was an accident, as accidental as the vodka that he had no choice but to guzzle. As accidental as the vomit that had raised up above his shoes. He didn't want to feel that way tonight.

A good sport, he finishes his dance moves and comes back to his friends at the table. He makes some inquiries into the rules for getting something into his stomach. After some satisfying answers, he says please and gets one of them to lift a half-shell to his lips, so he can slurp oyster meat into the bile of his stomach. The butter sauce is cilantro-driven and it makes the sides of his tongue become suddenly aware of themselves.

Yes, this night was going to be different. He takes a swig from each hand and says please for a bite of crab legs. The cheap plastic cracking sound opens up the spiny exoskeleton: juicy white red leg meat. He grabs it with his teeth, gentle but firm, and brings it into a dipping bowl, with a dog-like flourish, swirls it around the butter sauce before finally slurping the meat into his mouth. His stomach folds over on the seafood, and mashes it into one piece, marinating with the smooth bite of vodka.

The newness of the feeling starts to settle deep in his torso, the sensation of breaking past something old and catching something new at a hundred miles an hour, mouth open, catching endorphins between his teeth. He's becoming the same as everything else. The separations between him, the parts of him, and the objects and the people around him start to feel arbitrary, that there is nothing really holding him back from being these things, from drinking it all in, as it drinks him into its own mouth, his mouth.

His teeth shine as he asks his friends the difference between their atoms and his–nuzzling his face up next to theirs, asking what the difference is now, answering for them that there's really no distinction. He's a good sport and so are they. They humor him, give some consideration to his musings.

When it's finally time for a piss, he b-lines for the crowd, shouting about the chance to earn a quarter. One faithful friend stops him, pulls him back by the shoulders, and stabilizes him on the way to the bathroom.

The taped one breaks free, kicks himself up off a urinal, and sticks the landing, only spilling a few drops from his 40 bottles. His friend tells him to fucking stay still. The taped one giggles.

Fucking stay still.

And that's when it hits him. Why is it remarkable in any way for his friend to unzip his pants? For anyone on the floor to earn twenty-five cents? They're all the same atoms, aren't they? Are the protons in his hands any different from the protons in his pants?

Finally free, the taped one brings both hands down on the head and back of his friend, breaking the glass across his skin, across his own skin, cutting into the skin. Swirling. The blood is the same as the screaming. The vodka burning up the underside of the flesh, the same as eyes, lung tissue. In his head, he knows it's all the same, but to the eye, some things still hold their difference. There's separation between their ankles. The ceiling tile and the rib bones. More swirling. Swirling until the eyes can't tell the difference between things. Little bits come off, some cling on, like particles sticking faithfully to their nucleus orbit. Swirling, swirling. Screaming, both of them, all of them. All of them until they're the same as the piss on the floor. No vodka left. Only the fluorescent light that tastes like vodka.

But there's another coming in, a suit of skin still separate, brazen, not even feigning the appearance of unity. Not knowing where to grab, the new one only slides fingertips against the blood. Trying to help, poor guy. The skin isn't easy to grab. Eyes are screams in this bathroom. When another opens the door, the music is piss too. A couple comes in on a trip, and the unity on the floor is nothing but recreation, hallucinations. But, maybe they understand it, not like the last one to enter, now part of the skin too. The piss tells them to join.

Trusting their trip, they step into the glass shard teeth of the tile floor. The homogeneity hurts at first, the blood in their mouth pissing out music, light, more teeth, a reconstructed bottle of vodka, the skin, closing like a zipper, adhesive to seal them all in place, the crab meat too, brain oysters, carapace lungs, a couple just trying to fuck in the bathroom, a constant birth of them all.

KISSING AT THE FOOT OF THE BED

"The idea I kinda like and I kinda just keep coming back to is that we're Coney Island—but with demons. And I don't mean Coney Island in the literal sense, that there's a strong man lifting old-school dumbbells above his head or Ferris wheels with all the colorful lights. I just mean that it's a place where a city and its amusement park are one in the same thing. It just so happens that the thrills we offer are sleep paralysis demons.

So what does this mean for us? Well, we have to really really stress, I mean really drive it home for our audience, that this is something that is specific to our city. In our city only. That's an enormous value-prop for us. Because, folks, we are sitting on a massive opportunity here. We could be the first city, maybe in the last thousand years, to do this sort of storytelling. And since all the other agencies have fled the city—a little cowardly I think – we have a front-row seat on this thing.

And I don't want to think about it like we're the only ones with that front seat, even though we kind of already are. I want to crush this pitch to the city. We don't know how long this thing is going to last. If they like how we do this, then we can all provide plenty of job security for ourselves and our families. If the demon wave is over, and they really enjoyed working with us, then this could turn into a shitload of municipal accounts. And the amazing part about those is that the government fires no one. You land a government contract, and then no one is paid enough to care about whether or not you do a good job. But, of course, we're going to crush it for them.

So… let's get back to it. I really want to dive in deep on these ideas. Let's test them out and give each other meaningful feedback. Really want to bring our best to them tomorrow. I guess let's start with the idea of Coney Island in the amusement park. What are y'all's thoughts on that?"

An enormous clearing of the throat, half a forced cough, "We actually took a little bit of a different approach. Instead of the bright airy, abstract glow of Coney Island, we thought about rock 'n' roll. I mean, we've seen all these rock bands go all over the world making all kinds of money keeping demonic themes in the front row. They're still going strong, most of them! And we just happen to live in a city full of demons. Talk about demonic themes!

So instead of being in the air, like the thrill of an amusement park, demoniality brings you down into the dirt. All the way into hell. It's greedy. It's dangerous. And people want to be a part of it. It's a notch on your belt, that you can survive, and you can bring home the story.

And I'm not even advocating for one over the other. I say we do some A/B testing. Do you know if they're still interested in a billboard campaign? If they've got the budget for it, we can try out those ideas and try to do some research on who ends up visiting this summer. If it's a bunch of heads, then we know the danger-lovin' Rock 'n' Roll really stuck the landing. If we see a bunch of families sharing a hotdog, then we know the amusement park was what resonated. I mean, you could probably pitch them on the idea of doing both, right, even if it means raising their budget? Like you said, no one else is here."

The two interns drop their notepads on the empty conference room table. They bump their way down the hall and press the down-arrow of the skinny elevator. They laugh about how slow it's arriving. When it opens, they climb into the must of its nickel doors and red carpet. There's a squeal in the cables overhead and they can feel it between their ears.

In the basement, they almost have to duck because the asbestos ceiling hangs so low. The hallway winds and leads them to a defunct break room, gray tiles, and a twin bed. The furniture must've been here when the building was bought, but now most people are scared to fall asleep at work. The interns are pretty eager.

They're kissing at the foot of the bed. The paisley sheets are creasing under their weight. Over their frantic heads, pipes slosh water straight through themselves and rattle their way up to the floors above them. The walls radiate a fluorescent glow and it doesn't even match the only source of light which is a lamp with a soft orange glow in the corner.

One kisses the other's neck and asks, "Are you ready?"

Eyes closed, "Yes."

They throw themselves onto the bed and sink their faces into the pillows. Pull the blanket up to their throats.

"What do you think—if they come at all—what do you think they'll be?"

"The Feathers are more common. Probably one of them."

"No, just because they were the first to come doesn't mean they're more common. It's equal between them and the Pretty Faces."

"People inflate the number of Pretty Face sightings. It's the masks—they stand out more."

"They all stand out when they're at the foot of your bed."

"Not the Whisper Teeth."

"You know what I mean."

The intern rolls over, "Night."

"Goodnight."

The sound of deep breathing mixes with the sounds of the building. It's not long before they're both asleep.

One wakes up perfectly paralyzed. There's a visiting voice. It's wet, forced through something narrow. It's a Whisper Teeth speaking.

"Think I saw you at the standup. Maybe at the bagel shop too. There's a surprising amount of drifters at both. I want to tell you something now. I hope you're ready to hear it. This – all this – isn't something that you should want, that you should fuck with. You've got something sharp inside of you. It's broken and dripping with the bile of your stomach. When I see something like that. I wish it was me. The pop of something breaking. You can hear it. I don't get to do it as much as I would like. So when I see something fractured inside someone, I think about what it would have been like if it was me. You find yourself wondering that too. What it might be like to hurt someone. In a profound way, really hurt someone. And I hadn't planned to ask you this. This just has me thinking. Do you mind if I try it with you?"

STAND UP COMEDY!

The disco lights are off. Her suit is double the size it should be. A spotlight that could only be used in magic shows or stand-up comedy illuminates her presence on the stage. She's handing out afternoon punchlines. Recklessly pointing a microphone at her face, forgetting it's there half the time, holding it up to nothing, her roof-of-mouth voice becoming instantly quiet.

The crowd is sparse, not much more than Netti and the Mixing Boys, roaring the second she hits them with her opening line, "You ever had sex with a demon?"

It's a fair question. I sure as hell haven't, but it looks like some of my friends here on the front row they sure as fuck have fucked a demon. Am I right?

No, no I haven't had sex with a demon. But I know someone who has. My old college roommate, we were good friends. We both stayed in the city, got coffee from time to time, bitched about the man and our lives. Now, I wasn't always what you see before you now. I was the quiet one in college. And he was the slut. So, when I heard last year that a bunch of motherfuckers were seeing demons on the edge of their bed. I just knew that he was gonna fuck one of them!

But it wasn't as hot as you might think, you perverts. The little demon got confused, see. They don't have sex where they come from. So, naturally, it was confused by the idea. The closest thing it had seen to sex in its time here on this plane is CPR. Which is why, when my friend had laid down, the stupid motherfucker started giving him chest compressions! And, ladies, that might do it for you – I'm not here to judge. But, fellas, don't get any ideas. So, me and my friend, we like to decompress about such things. And the best we could figure is this.

We all know about this city we call home. We've all stepped over an overdose victim on the way to work."

The Mixing Boys roar, like they've heard this joke already, one of their favorites. Netti laughs along, sinks a little into his coat. The comedian reminds him of Steph–the hardwon assertiveness. Steph didn't have it when they were kids, but he'd bet she's carved it out for herself by now.

She goes on, "Now, some of you are from out of town. And you might not like that last joke. But let me let you in on a little something. You spend your whole life wondering what you'd do in a situation like this. A chance to save someone. To be a hero! And what you may not expect is that you won't disappoint your younger self," she whispers with absurd quiet, "for once!"

The comedian does a robotic dance number, holding her microphone up to her knuckles, elbows, and shoulders, popping the joints for the room to hear. Four beats and she's back at the microphone.

"The first OD victim you see, you shout OH MY GOD NOTIFY THE PARAMEDICS. And you pump, pump, pump against that scrawny little chest until help arrives.

What you might be disappointed to hear is that it only takes about a week of doing this shit every morning until you're like OH MY GOD CAN'T YOU JUST CALL THEM YOURSELF?! And in about a month, you'll walk around them, and you might not even notice, my friends. Just like a puddle, or an Open sign at a bagel shop you've always wanted to try but you know you'll never actually step foot in the establishment, no not once. You just kinda throw up your hands and go OHSHIT and walk right on by, you calloused motherfucker.

But I get it. I get why anyone does drugs in this city. Every night for the Last. Eight. Months. I've had a demon sitting on the foot of my bed. And you're all probably wondering what demon it is. Let's hear some guesses from the crowd!" She raises a hand to her ear.

"Feather!"

"Feather!"

"BITCH!"

"Feather!"

Netti looks over at who called her that, hating the way that man moves his thinly bearded jaw. He hopes the comedian can make it out of this fucking city.

Well, here I am thinking you were a bunch of balls-for-brains sitting in a damn near empty disco club at four in the afternoon listening to some stand-up comedy. But I stand CORRECTED. Yes, Yes, I'm a Featherhead. I know that's not a shock for most people. And I'm not ashamed. I know what it means to attract Feathers. I do it on a nightly basis after all. And it's not all bad actually. I've come to expect it'll be there, waiting for me in the middle of the night once I've been frozen out of my sleep. I'm so used to it now that I'd probably offer it a backrub if I wasn't paralyzed. Least I could do after it started giving me foot rubs a couple months back.

Now, now. I know that sounds nice. But remember the demon who gave my friend CPR instead of a good rail? Well, imagine the foot rub! Let me tell you what it's like.

It takes my foot in its hand and starts to trace the lines on the bottom with its finger. Now, realize that its finger is wet one hundred percent of the time. Not too sure what that means in demon land but I'm pretty sure it's a good sign. I STILL GOT IT."

Netti whips his hands around above his head, "Hell yeah, you do!" And his face clouds with regret.

The comedian can't hear anything around her. She doesn't break momentum, "The only real way to describe it is that it's like a palm reading on my foot. And as much as this fucker is reading my foot, I bet it could tell me the Powerball numbers if it could only speak!

But I carry on just like the rest of you. I wake up, get my ass out of bed, and go to work. And as you probably put together by now, comedy is not my day job. Otherwise, I wouldn't be here, right now, talking to twelve of you on volunteer wages. I'm on paid time off right now, for crying out loud! I told my boss I needed to go get some experience, and that this would help launch my artistic career. And the worst part is that he believes in me. Gave me all the PTO when I ran out earlier this year doing a circuit, again, for zero pay.

So, I just wanted to say thank you. Thank you for being here. Thank you for being drunk as fuck, for laughing at all my jokes but missing every single punchline. Laughing like fucking idiots who have no idea what's going on. Do you think my city's funny? Do you find it hilarious that a demon likes to sit at the edge of my bed? Fuck you. Fuck you and your wrinkled-up little ticket for one drunken ass disco comedy hour. You piece of shit."

Netti can't hear anything around him. He's robbing the pocket of a Mixing Boy, pulling out two pills tossing them into his mouth under the disguise of a cough. They taste dry and sharp and the room feels like a throat swallowing them whole.

Between the afternoon and night, the air in the disco feels thick and quiet. Glasses clink behind the bar, cleaned, and left to dry in the artificial light. The Mixing Boys pass a toy pipe around their circle. It spits out bubbles when you blow it between your teeth and they make a scene of popping each one. Netti sits at a bar stool, tapping his fingers—the motion tinged with boredom and touches of hate and resignation. After the comedian trudged off stage, he'd joined the group to stretch his legs, but their every sentence had been spoken before. The sounds of their conversation hurt the edges of his brain. He thinks of the city beyond the walls of the disco, and he thinks of the city inside this building–how it'll feel different tomorrow. He'll run with the boys again, on and into misery and feeling fucked and waiting by the bar with no one beside him, waiting to re-enter the circle. To pass the toy pipe. Inhale the plastic and taste chemicals on his tongue.

This is how he passes the hour until the business district vomits up a crowd and covers the dancefloor. The bar's packed tight with new bodies, each one absorbing the sound of a bassline with their thigh-highs and jackets. Netti's planted at the end in his same seat, drawing wolf detective variations on the backs of napkins. The cartoon's teeth snapping at a martini straw. Sneaking in the shadows. Shining a flashlight off his fangs to reveal a tangle of thieves hiding in the corner of a bathroom with the lights shot out.

From the corner of his eye, he sees the marketing agency enter the club. They're snaking around in a cha-cha line, right to left with forward motion. Their leader, the Vest, is at the front and he's smiling, believing this moment of team-building is working, really working. Netti stacks his napkins neatly on top of each other and presses down until they're completely flat under his palms. A deep breath. Then off to the dance floor.

His drawings left to flash their teeth at the bar.

He twists around a man in a coconut bra and firecrackers braided into his beard. Hops between two women swinging bony arms like jump ropes. His fur coat brushes past their jaws and they laugh over the music. Momentum only stops when he collides with a wall of backs circled around the center of the dancefloor. He tries shoving between them but they're all too eager, cheering for what's in the middle of them all. Only glimpses for Netti, straps, poles, yards of fabric boasting intolerable patterns. Whoops and shouts spit from the crowd. Dancers bend their necks back, watching as a man on stilts is hoisted above their heads, reaching all the way to the disco ball.

The Stilt Walker stretches his arms into the light, steadies himself, and begins to move. The crowds split around his legs as he ducks under the purple glow of the disco ball. Some dodge his steps with cartoonish close calls while others fall to the floor in mock terror, their best impression of a monster movie character about to get their brains crushed by the beast. There are dive rolls between legs. Pole dancing, weightless grinding on the stilts. The man above them all screams the words to the wrong song, smiling, blinded by disco lights, marching long-legged through the center of the dancefloor.

Netti takes one last weary, amused look at the scene and makes his way to the bar where the marketing team has fortified their presence. They're arranging and rearranging the order of the napkins with the wolf cartoons, sliding the images around like a game of Three Card Monte. Without saying hello, Netti squeezes his head between two of their torsos and watches his story get rearranged on the surface of the bar. He watches for several rounds of reordering, and the sequence usually closes with images that involve the most amount of teeth. Netti catches himself not minding how they fuck up his work. With his hands in the pockets of his fur coat, he asks himself why. Why he's so okay with their version of things.

Thirty feet behind him, there's a drug deal taking place. A person in a leopard print getup pulling a plastic bag out of their cleavage, handing it to a bookish type who clearly feels uncomfortable in the sequins covering his body.

That's when the hands of a Mixing Boy yank Netti back into a head-lock. Another dips his fingers in a drink, then flicks droplets of iridescent martini into Netti's face, shouting, "I christen you in the name of the Father, the Mother, and their Bastard Child, Netti!"

The alcohol on his face smells acidic and he imagines little angry jaws from deep in his chest rising up his throat and out of his mouth to devour each drop. He wipes the rainbow droplets off his face with the sleeve of his coat. There's a knot of bodies around him, the marketing team, the Mixing Boys. Out of the corner of his eye, he sees Castra moving in a far orbit around them. She stalks closer and closer to Leopard Print and Sequin Boy.

The Vest tries to quiet down the two groups as they shoot the shit at a raucous volume, strangers in the Disco trading lines about work and city-wide violence. Netti squirms his way to the outer curve of their circle, licking a drop of martini that had hidden itself in the corner of his lips.

"Okay, okay, you fucking animals. I can see the night's off to a good start," he laughs with a hollow, chesty laugh. "So I'm going to civilize things a little with a toast."

In a backroom, the Masked Killer slices down a high tipper drenched in Malbec. Blood careens down his chest and under his belt. The Killer steps in the puddle and opens the backroom door. Tonight's mask is woven tight with gauze and cheap plastic beads from a jewelry kit. The look is bright and compliments the fluids running along the edge of the blade. The Killer's at the edge of the dancefloor now, not far off from the bar, but covered by the dense knot of dancers between them.

At the bar, the Vest's toast is gaining some momentum, "The thing about this city is this. That it rewards the bold and the ballsy. Those who stick around have an enormous bounty to reap, practically a damn dead elk just dropped on their table by the village hunting team. We could have left with the other agencies–and, to the Mixing Boys, I'm sure you could have done the same with other studios–but we stayed. We stayed. And there will be a reward for that. Even on the down days, the ones that don't seem to have a direction–"

The Killer slips the blade between two vertebrae. The dancer bends sideways into a crescent shape before falling soundlessly to the floor. Another gets a slash to the sternum, only enough to break skin and club the bone, a dense thud. The dancer falls back, attempts to run but the Killer swings the blade across both his hamstrings. The movement makes a meaty sound and the victim vomits up a clump of feathers.

Netti doesn't hear a word the Vest is saying. Doesn't see the Killer either. He's watching Castra close in on the Sequin Boy. The Leopard Print's made it off the floor out of sight, but it's too late for their buyer. Castra's got a boxcutter.

"So, as we're drinking tonight. And I have a feeling this is the first of many drinks," he raises the volume of his voice, seeing that he's losing the eyes of the Mixing Boys. The attention of his employees was gone when he first cleared his throat. "Just remember that we—"

From behind, Castra swipes the boxcutter down Sequin Boy's earlobe. He turns around with his mouth gaped and a braid of blood down his neck. She leaves him with a shallow slice under his rib and makes her way to the exit. Sequin Boy's on his knees, holding his ear with both hands as his torso bleeds through the outfit that he hated to put on before the club.

The Killer's getting closer to the Stilt Walker.

"—are the ones who stayed. God. Dammit." The Vest throws his glass into the air. They all watch as it rises, falls, and shatters across the tiles.

The Stilt Walker can't see the bodies from up there. It's too bright and the rising heat has stung his eyes with sweat. He bumps into the disco ball with the back of his head. Stabilizes, again. With fingers splayed wide, he starts to fondle the disco ball and the mirrors continue to blind him.

The Killer isn't focused on his violence, chopping down bodies just to have a path to walk. Most don't notice they're about to get the blade. Others know what's coming and they wag their bodies in the purple light before the kill stroke. The last one goes down with their nose cut inward through their skull.

The Killer rests, a moment, at the feet of the Stilt Walker. Netti can see it from the bar. His jaw loosens, in a little amazement at what's about to happen.

The Killer begins to climb.

He grabs the pant legs by the handful, slides his legs up one of the stilts. Moves with smoothness all the way to the top, until his feet are on the Stilt Walker's feet—the two of them swaying at the top of the Disco. The Stilt Walker's screaming with revelry, clearly assuming the Killer as an exuberant participant. But, the Killer thrusts the blade under his jaw.

The point of the blade emerges triumphantly from his open mouth. His eyes roll back in the lights, shaking only as the Killer begins to pull. Hands tugging back on the blade, then the arms. Frustrated, the Killer begins to pull with his whole convulsing body until something loosens. One side of the jaw breaks, giving an inch before the entire thing rips off from the Stilt Walker's skull.

Together, they're falling. Knocking into the disco ball with both their bodies, dislodging it from the club ceiling. The disco ball crashes to the floor first. The crowd rushes to the broken object, stepping around Sequin Boy's body, flailing from the shards that have flown into his face. They examine what could be fixed, what mirrors need to be replaced and which ones could be glued back together, swearing that this is the kind of shit they deal with now. Netti works into the crowd, arm to arm with his Mixing Boys and the marketing team. As he's jostled around, he can't seem to care, can't feel what he's seeing on all their faces. He's only glad he remembered the napkin drawings, stashing them in his coat pocket, folding them over and over, inward toward himself and inward toward himself again.

Behind them, the Killer and the Stilt Walker slam to the floor. But, it only takes a moment. The Killer leaves the body behind, walking up to the loose jaw, a silhouette on the purple light-up tiles. Then, it's more from the blade. The first few swings spray blood from the jaw, but only last so long. Then teeth are released, knocked into the air with chips of jawbone. Swing after swing. Until the floor's covered in loose teeth.

KEEP THE CAGE ROLLING

Netti latches onto a group that he saw in the bagel shop, weighing down their stomachs for the long night ahead. Later, at the Disco, he times it just right–pulls out a room-temp bagel and tosses it to a man with an embroidered hat. The group concurs that Netti's made of magic.

"Funny you should ask that. You see, my father was actually a detective. And while I tend to be pretty agnostic when it comes to the whole nature/nurture bullshit, I am self-aware enough to know that his career has had a big influence on me. I'd even go so far as to say it's a big reason I follow demons to keep myself busy with the demon-stalking. There's a shit ton of them, as you can see. But there are nuanced ways of doing it that require a lot more skill than you'd think. Or, at least, a lot more than I originally thought. Take the Pretty Faces for example, there's a fuck ton of 'em. Compared to the others at least."

The conversation, against all odds, continues on the dance floor. He feels close enough now–the borderline where he measures on nights like this and steps over with confidence and a charming amount of recklessness–close enough to lean into their ears and shout his stories.

"It wasn't like that. My father always said I was a beautiful boy. That I would heal the world with— he called it— my great black hole of feeling, like no skin on earth could keep its shape around the void. And he meant it in a good way too, said he wasn't sure where I got it from. He and my mom were always at each other's throats, and others' too. When I ate all the drugs in the city, I don't think that's what he had in mind. But here

I am, clean for more than a year, and tailing demons into alleys and even people's houses. When I really think about it. Like when I stop and just think. The pain is pretty unbearable."

He checks again after checking only seconds ago. He loves the weight of it. This one dyed with a crushed powder of some kind. The mask hidden in his coat pocket.

"You know, people used to make love at the Disco. And I'm not just talking about promiscuity, though there was plenty of that too, and that's all fine and good. But I'm talking about people actually making love at the Disco. But things are different now. People go, and they drink and they dance and then they go home—maybe a quick fuck somewhere in there, nothing fancy. And they go to sleep, knowing a demon'll stroke their hair in an hour or two. No love. A making love-less Disco.

He thinks about a time he vomited in his friend's car, struggled to get the window down in time and hurled onto the inside of the door. Some of the chunks got into the creases of the leather stitching and never came out, not in the time he knew the guy at least. Netti wonders if the floor is the same way. Vomit chunks of people's insides dried up in the cracks.

"My dad, he wasn't just a detective for his job. But he was a detective nut too. He'd seen every movie, could recognize Humphrey Bogart's chin from a mile away, I'm sure. And he loved all of them—the British, the French, the Americans. But he always told me that all the smarts in the world can't land a punch like your fist. So he always came back to the hardboiled detectives, the ones with the square jaws and leather shoes, the last ones who really knew how to be graceful with a phone cord. I'm serious, the way they'd hang up the phone with the femme fatale. It's not the same. The way we say goodbye to each other now. No confidence, no knowing we'll see them soon. No six shooters coming out of your sock. No punching your way to the secret or a tight-lipped kiss at the end. No, nothing like that."

The sunrise does its best that morning as they leave the club in the rain.

They'd been tasked with a bottle episode. A story confined to a locked room, usually saved for shows on budgetary watch. Less relevant to animated series. But, nonetheless, the Director's orders would be passed down from the Mixing Boys and across the hall to Netti and all the other inbetweeners. The idea was that the wolf would have to figure out which of the ladies locked up in a ski lodge lobby had taken the key.

But the gag was that they all had stolen the key. Netti sketched frames of them sliding the key to one another with their fluffy tails and he'd draw out the illusion of snowfall in the enormous window behind them, that during the day must have been a view from high up on the mountain, but, at night, it was a place for sleeping far from any of the city lights in the distance.

Faster, they pass the key, and with more daring, even going so far as to pass it off as a gold ring on their paws as they speak with the wolf detective. And it keeps getting faster. It's absurd. It's almost no time at all before they're passing the key to each other so quickly that it begins to levitate behind their backs. Orbiting the room with the wolf detective at its center. He's asking questions of the others. They're giving him witty answers, but their expressions aren't as tongue-in-cheek as the viewer would expect. They're not sly, only knowing. Like someone whose situation is so dire that lying to stay alive is as involuntary as breathing or heating up by the ski lodge fireplace.

The key starts to bleed. Blood streaming thinly around its stem. It's screaming too, but it sounds like the wind. Only the wolf who first hid the key notices. She sheds a tear and it clings a small clump of fur to her face. One of the other wolves notices her pain and reaches to comfort her.

This time, the detective notices. They close the circle and cluster around to pat her on the back. And that's when he sees the key flying in its full circle, hears it screaming. He turns to the camera and the next episode is solidly in place.

Unconsciously, Netti mumbles the title to himself, "The Case of the Weeping Key." One of the Mixing Boys makes a comment that he seems pretty introspective for an artist at the Disco.

"So much output all day," Netti points to his skull, "you gotta fill it up with something."

"That's what we're all saying, but you don't see any of us sitting on the bench and staring at the wall."

"I'm disparaging your art, but it's a different kind of work."

"No shit, that's what art is, you asshole. Not everything is a tapestry of a unicorn or a statue of a wood nymph. Of course it's different."

"So it makes people tired in different ways."

"I, for one, find it cathartic."

"Mixing colors all day?"

"It's better than an infinite number of positions between points A and B. That wolf must have really done it all by now."

"He's definitely found himself in some pickles."

"You've been there the whole time? Since the pilot?"

"Why are you asking me that?"

"I was curious, have you?"

"No, but you know the answer. That's why I'm asking."

"It's just a question, Netti."

"You were there before me. All of you."

"I'm just feeling you out," the Mixing Boy smiles.

"What's your point of reference?"

"The way you talk about things and how they bleed over time."

"You're going to have be more fucking specific with what you're trying to say."

"That's what I'm doing now. I'm about to show you."

Netti bows apologetically, with a mock gesture of go-on-then.

"You know our work, that colors aren't the end of it. That we spend a lot of time in the basement."

"That's where the boss likes to keep you," Netti pops an elbow forward for a vaudeville nudge.

"The boss is in the basement."

"Sexy."

"It's not."

"You'd have to convince me otherwise."

"You've never met the boss?"

"Only impressions, that I've heard. Intro music. That's all."

"She's not what you'd expect."

"I only hold loose ideas of expectation when it comes to studio bosses and the basements they frequent."

"You're gonna love her."

"You and I aren't always on the same page."

"What are you talking about? We've gotten on pretty well all these nights."

"You know I'm not a Mixing Boy," Netti smiles with a euphoric pain across his face.

"No, Netti. You precede the Mixing Boys. We're just the return of who you used to be. All of us. All at once. We're the same person at different times."

"You're starting to sound like one of my ramblings."

"That's what I'm saying."

"I can't believe that, my friend," Netti looks to the disco ball through the cracked door, shattered on the floor tiles, "We're all more separate than you could possibly imagine."

"I'm willing to bet on it."

"Well, we could start with our common ground of a shared boss."

"I think she's gonna love me."

"She's only ever mentioned one inbetweener. And she spoke fondly of his garish fur coat."

At the mixing counter, a purple-boxed cracked-to-hell record player breaks in a newly released twelve-inch. There's a low rumbling down the stairs that Netti's never heard over the roar of furious sketching, painting, and mile-long trails of creative feedback. The frequency feels nice between Netti's eyes.

Netti thinks of bingo when he sees the demons. The Mixing Boys standing at the helm of a three-man crank, turning a bingo roller the size of a closet, its cage rattling in front of a storyboard plastered to the basement wall. On the inside, there's a dark weight turning around in the roller, sinking in the bottom, nearly falling at the top of the turn, locked to its spot on the cage by nothing other than nauseous momentum. The Mixing Boys move their arms with near silent power as the clank of the rattle buries the heft of their breathing. There's a lounge chair in the corner, a woman slouched with a joint between her knuckles, her eyes trailing the circular motions of the roller, trailing them so intensely it's like she's causing them to happen, rotation after rotation. She breaks her gaze to wave Netti over. He comes closer, adjusts his fur coat. The roller spins faster.

The woman pulls her hair back from her face at the same instant it covers over her expression again, "Hi, you're the inbetweener, aren't you?"

"The fast one, yeah."

"How many sheets a day?"

"For me, it's more about the movements of the wolf than the number of sheets. That, and I don't count my sheets."

"That's bad business. How am I supposed to exploit your creativity if we can't assign a number to your production?"

"Maybe we could make an episode about it. The wolf gets to the bottom of what it means to depict the removal of ceiling tiles and map out imaginary air-conditioning ducts to sneak through in the night."

She points to the storyboard, "Might as well."

Now that he's standing closer to the rolling cage, he suddenly can't tell how long he's been down in this basement.

She plants the joint between her teeth, digs down into the lounge chair to pull out a thick marker, tosses it to him, "I'm serious, draw it up."

"What about—"

"Just tear it down. There's a fresh sheet underneath," she pulls a bottle of dark liquor from some folds in the cushions of the chair.

Black ink, that moments ago was a series of panels with animated scenes inside, seeps between his fingers as he rolls the sheet into a sphere as big as his head. The new blank sheet is monolithic on the wall. He starts with the air ducts in thick lines, then sketching out the building around it, transforming the ducts, from a path of lines into the deep insides of a towering structure. By the end of his first sketches, the duct system is a labyrinth across the sheet. From her chair, the Director tilts the liquor bottle between her teeth. He scribbles the wolf inside the complex. From there, the story unfolds in every direction the ducts lead—all paths at the same time. The character arcs and actions and all the motions in between them fill up the structure to its edges. He's done with the episode.

The Mixing Boys are slowing down, losing momentum in their work to keep the cage rolling. The Director stoops down to the floor, lifting the crumbled mass of old storyboard paper to her chest, bows her head over the armful, and lets half a bottle of liquor fall slowly from her mouth and soak into the paper. The orb soaks in the liquid, wilting into a small version of itself. The Mixing Boys, setting their leader on her knees, begin to step back from their work, taking her posture as an invitation to rest. Netti can almost see what the dark shape inside the cage is as it slows down. The Director's reaching behind her ear, pulling out her still-embered joint; it's singed small strands of her hair and sent dark curls of smoke into a semi-circle around her head. She drops the joint onto the paper ball. A few seconds seem to pass, then it's all in flames. She manages to hold it until large pieces begin falling off, like pieces of decomposed skin that a body has rejected. That's when she throws it at the boys, and when it hits them it bursts open, little ashes clinging onto their arms and their shirts. They stomp at the flames once or twice before she clubs the nearest one with her liquor bottle. Glass shards fall to the floor with the rest of the bottle's contents where it immediately alchemizes into flames. Unmanned, the roller goes from full rotations to swinging its dark weight up on one end before it falls to the other, back and forth until it's clear what's inside. As the Mixing Boys, in flames, run past him, Netti makes out two Feather demons in the cage, sick with perpetual motion, the bodies swollen around the bars of the cage. There are screams from the boys, but Netti can't stop looking at the demons. They're misshapen, the momentum of the cage having blurred the shape of their bodies into something else. But, the more he looks, the oddness wears off. They start to look like any other Feather he's seen. And then he realizes they're reforming, returning to their original shape.

The Director pulls the fur coat from Netti's shoulders and goes after the Mixing Boys. With some cursing, she's gotten one to the floor where she can beat down the flames with Netti's coat. Several of the others that have already rolled off the flames are helping stomp out the burning of their friend. It's what seems like a few minutes of cooling off, catching breath. And then they're back to work, their arms slick with superficial burns.

It's not long before the wheel is back at full speed. They're struggling, and Netti thinks of helping them, but he also thinks of his arms rubbing against them, their skin rubbed away one transparent layer at a time, his sweat causing the torn skin to stick to his own arms. He thinks of swatting away these sheets of skin, how they would probably just stick to his palms until they stuck somewhere else on his body, and he would carry their burn wounds around on his own flesh. He'd have to run upstairs and pour a bottle of vodka over his arms, something to scour the foreign matter off of him. If that didn't work, he might even have to light it on fire, briefly. Just long enough to eat up those little chunks of skin. He'd be prepared, not like them.

The Director sits next to him on the enormous chair. Both of them watching the wheel turn, the demons inside held down tight against the grates by the speed of the mechanism.

She hooks an arm around his shoulder, "It's nice to meet you, Netti."

He recognizes something about her touch. It's neighborly, and clearly capable of violence. He understands the source of the former. The latter, he struggles to pinpoint. He thinks back on his own violence, imagines wrapping his own arm around himself while wearing a rubber mask full of razor blades. His imaginary arm shrieks from his own touch, pulls away with a mouthful of shallow gashes. It's not himself. He can feel, in her, something that resembles the havoc of the entire city.

"And nice to finally meet you, Director," he clears his throat, slides out from underneath her arm, "I really enjoyed the direction of the last episode. Really smart angle."

"You'll have to remind me, Netti. They all blend together. Glad to hear it, nonetheless."

"The Case of the Rabid Clam."

"Eh, I'm not sure we earned the ending."

"What are you talking about? It was all right there in the opening shot; I drew it. It was the Clam Farmer the whole time."

"Oh, well I fucking know that. We earned it on paper. But, I'm not sure we sold it on emotional impact. And, the thing is, I think you know that. And… I think I know why you're not talking any shit right now, not even to impress me."

"There could be an argument…"

She holds her hand flat beside his eyes, shielding his view from the Mixing Boys.

He continues, "…that the color scheme wasn't quite there, during the last episode. The last episode only."

"What was it, then? What shade?"

"The eyes of the Oyster Farmer. Green. Green was right. But, they were moss green. They should have been harlequin. The frame of the final reveal when he turns around in the shadows, that could have sold it. That would have been the episode."

"Now," she drops her forehead against his, pointing her own green eyes at his, "you know why I'm so fucking hard on these boys."

Netti can hear a roll of gauze unwinding. It's like he can feel the temperature lowering on his own skin as they open a box of burn ointment, arguing on how to do it and who should endure the treatment first. He attempts to keep score of their back-and-forth as the Director goes on.

"We're all just eager little audience members, Netti. And what really gets us going is the Reveal. And what's so fucking annoying about detectives is that they're always trying to force life into this heavily greased plot funnel all so that the whole stiff body can pop out of the other side a little thinner and wearing a new expression that tells you exactly who's been knifing everybody down. All that, just for a moment of revelation. But, what they're all too dick-brained about to realize is that life is at the top of the funnel, and so is the Reveal. All just circling around at the top, never quite going down the hole if you don't force gravity to do its job."

"I'm not sure I agree though," he hesitates. "I'm not just an inbetweener. I'm a detective too."

She responds, "Ah, enough bullshit, Netti. Not sure what the hell you're saying but I've got some shit to show you."

He pulls his coat a little tighter around his shoulders.

"When I was a kid, I was a big fan of caviar. Mama would bring it back from all her work travels. So much so that anytime she left the door, even just to leave for an everyday shift, I'd sometimes ask her for an orange spoonful, but usually the green ones. I called them butterballs. Isn't that fucking stupid?

So, one day, naturally I asked where butterballs were made. She laughed and didn't go to work for another week, just disappeared into her back room every morning—until one day, she came out with her fingers wrapped around a fishing pole and a filet knife pointing out of her jean pocket. We were going to make butterballs.

And when I finally caught the little fucker, I'd never wanted so badly to see something dead in my life. Not until that moment, and not even since then. And I've wanted to see some bastards burn in my work. But the emptiness of its gills and the perfect circles of its eyes, it might as well have been made out of plastic. She was foolish enough to think I'd be repulsed by what came next. No, it was the falsity that repulsed me; I was relieved to see my mother slide the blade through its scales. And that's when I saw it. Those putrid little yellow eggs, sliding out from between the slit that Mama made. Falling to the dock, splatting into an ungatherable pile of insides. She pointed eagerly, saying look, look, these are butterballs. But, I already knew. I saw this coming before she dropped a hook in the water. All I said was that butterballs were green, and if they weren't green they were orange.

I'm not like my mother, Netti. So I'm not going to show you something that you already know and make a big show of it, pointing to the Reveal like my whole existence as your mother depends on it. No, this is all top of funnel shit."

By now, she's dragging one of the Feathers out of its spinning cage. The body's mishappen, swollen on one side, so much so that the other side is near emptiness. The momentum of the wheel having pushed all its inner contents to one side of the demon's body. She starts between the eyes.

Sinks the tip of a filet knife through the cartilage-rich area, tugging, sawing, thrusting. Until one dull ripping sound emerges, followed by a dry slice, as she runs the blade down the feathers neck and body and far past its hips with a single movement of the blade. Feathers the color and consistency of motor oil spill out, dark, iridescent. They gush over her fingers, sliding along the curves of her bones and wrap around her wrist until they drip, pooling on the floor.

There's a moment when she's waiting. Waiting for hands to sweep in and gather the feathers, guide the flow into a bucket, scrape the inner flesh for any excess feathers stuck together by moisture. But there are no hands; those hands are tending to their minor burn wounds. She gathers the feathers herself, slopping them into a spare bucket that had been leaned against the wall. They fill it quickly and she's off to a ladder; she climbs to an orange glowing light, twists at the mechanism holding it in place and begins to lower it down close to the floor, illuminating a darkly smudged area of once-polished concrete. There, she slowly pours the gelatinous mass of feathers across the surface, coruscating under the light as it undulates up and down as if it were still pumping through the body of a demon.

When it starts to feel like her work is done for a while, she looks up at Netti, "Pretty soon, it'll be dry and we can smoke that shit."

GRIMOIRE RADIO – CALL #1

"Good morning, Murder City. Welcome to Grimoire Radio, home of your strangest, most harrowing experiences with the visiting demons. Feathers, Pretty Faces, Whisper Teeth. I'm DJ Calling Card, and I'm here to hear you out on all of it. Today's caller's got something a little fishy for us.

Go ahead, demon whisperer. Tell us what happened."

"Hi, I'm Flo. Long time listener. First time caller. And I wanted to tell you about my experience with a Feather Demon and my personal practice of mind displacement.

And I know how that sounds–very of the Age and spooky–but what I do is a little different than you might think. See, I like to bring an element of place into my spiritual practice. That's why I incorporated Sea-Monkeys.

I came across an ad, or an article in the paper, I'm not sure which, and I became enamored with how they can essentially freeze their life to survive unlivable conditions.

I don't think I need to explain the appeal of this to you.

So, when I finally got my package in the mail and let all those little eggs go into the water, I waited patiently for them to hatch. And then I began my work."

"Flo, we're loving this. We're loving you. But, are you gonna tell us about the demon you saw?"

"Well, if you want to separate the experience from the context, then I suppose we can discuss it in a vacuum. It was a Feather Demon. People say they don't know why these visitors come to their bed, and I can't speak for them, but mine came for the Sea-Monkeys.

I spent weeks concentrating on those little creatures. And part of me felt bad for this, but I was transferring their energy into my mind. Displacing their cryostasis into my own form. And you know it was working because the Feather Demon would show up, seemingly to syphon this essence from me. It would show up in my room, swirling its feathers around in its sockets, as I meditated through my processes. It was a beautiful demon—deep, deep blue plumage in its eyes. I even grew a little fond of its presence.

But, as I practiced the displacement of energies, something new happened, something I'd never seen in my years of practice."

"Flo, I hate to interrupt you, baby. But, you have to let us in on the good stuff."

"Well, that's precisely it. The good stuff. The three of us underwent a partial transfer of physical states.

I felt nothing, which was unusual. And I heard a slight crunching. And, you may think that sounds ominous, but it was actually quite pleasant. The small harsh sounds, lilting into my ears.

I looked up and it was my beautiful demon. But, the process had altered its face. Where there were once regal blue feathers, there were a million microscopic legs packed tight into its eye sockets. The sea-monkeys had been transferred from the tank and into the skull of the demon."

"Be serious, Flo."

"I'm dead serious, DJ Calling Card. That's why my eyes were in the sea-monkey tank. Lifeless, un-beautiful. And I hope you don't mind me being crass on the radio, but they immediately made me think of severed testicles. It was rotten seeing my eyes elsewhere."

"Flo, darling…"

"I know, I know. But, this is where I let you in on my story. That's what happened to them. This is what happened to me.

I have new eyes now. No eyes, really. Just beautiful feathers. They're so soft and they also hold the perfect level of dampness. I find myself glued to the mirror. Can't look away from myself. My beautiful blues.

The only reason I ever stop staring at my reflection is feeling them with my own fingers. When I touch them, there's no pressure, no crunch. Just the feeling of sinking. Dipping my fingers until they bump against my eye sockets."

"Flo, Flo, Flo, we're out of time, my dear. But, thank you for sharing, dear friend. And, to the rest of you, thank you for listening. Be sure to call us with your own stories sometime. I'm DJ Calling Card. Here's that shit you won't shut up about–it's Sister Sledge!"

HALLOWEEN: RUBBER TEETH

I had this mask when I was a kid, smelled terrible—put it on and it was like you were pulling yourself through a wormhole to some sort of hot, rotting planet. Great look though. The absolute snarl of a werewolf about to decapitate a villager in just a bite or two. Spent a lot of time that October working the word "lycanthrope" into my everyday conversations. If someone mentioned the head of the trailer park, I wished a lycanthrope would tear his ass up. I'd overhear the kids talking shit about who had the strongest dad, and I cut in saying that it didn't matter because a lycanthrope could kill both at once. I was dangerous. I could eat people.

So, my plan was this. I'd join my friends for trick-or-treating and make a haul on the first neighborhood. Drop off the pillowcase-full at my place on the way to our own roads. That's where I'd really have my wolf moment. See, the plan was for me to go on a little rampage, run around like a dog on the loose, spill some candy, maybe even scare some of the younger kids. It was Halloween. It was gonna be great.

And the fun part was that I didn't let anyone else in on the plan either. There were about six of us, the usual little coven, grabbing criminal amounts of candy out of all the plastic bowls. None of them knew. And none of them noticed when I ducked behind a double-wide that sat between a clearing of tall grass and the rest of the trailer park. The grass around it threatened to overtake and reach through the windows, growing even taller the further you looked into the clearing.

I pulled my mask up to take a breath, and listened out for whatever else may be around. And I could hear the family on their front porch, swirling around in their costumes, the call to say "cheese," and the flash of a camera. They were off to the races; the kids ran ahead and the two parents walked not far behind. And that's when a fucking cricket hopped down from the grass–that's how tall the grass was; it was hopping down, not up–and it landed right on my teeth. So, of course, I'm all "Fuck this," and "fuck your six-legged mother," and on and on and on.

And of course the dad heard me, so he started walking my way. I could tell he couldn't see me, wearing a big stupid necromancer cape over a tank top and blue jeans. With each step his arms would emerge from the cloth around his shoulders, showing all these swollen, water-logged tattoos of barbed wire and scorpion tails. There was something inside me–I couldn't really tell you where this came from–but I loathed this man. The way he slicked his hair back against his skull, his expression snarled all tough at the corner of his mouth, the half-ass costume. It was like a switch had flipped in my brain as soon as I saw him and thought he must have been the biggest fucking degenerate in our park, or really any other for that matter.

But I wasn't going to wait around until we could make eye contact. So I turned around on my belly and army-crawled through the grass. Less like a wolf, and more like the first little slime tube that crawled out of the ocean and onto the earth. But, I was moving. The dad was calling out "who's there," and demanding I come out. But I could tell by the sound of his voice that the distance between us was growing. All until I knocked the hell out of my forehead. I was dazing, rolled over and saw that I'd run into a shed.

The dad's voice was getting closer and I could hear that slight scraping sound of walking through really thick grass. My head was absolutely killing me, but there was really nothing to do but keep crawling. So, I sort of made my way round the corner and saw there was a loose sheet of paneling on that side. Just big enough for me to slime tube my way inside.

I hadn't realized how much the bugs and the grass had been getting to me until I was in such a dark, wet place. It was like an old cave was breathing all over me. It was nice, cooling off, listening to that dad get further and further away, giving up and moving on. It felt old, like this mud was from somewhere…else. Not really sure what it was about it. No form to it, just a bunch of muck under the shed. Except for this one small shape. A perfect little square. When my hand ran over it, I picked it up and shook it. Something was inside. Something with edges on it. The sound was crisp and it almost sounded like the steps of someone running, or beating a door down.

So I pulled myself into the long grass to look at what I'd found. It was a brand new box of razor blades. A little one, just a handful of blades inside. So, of course, my first thought was that this was going to take my rampage to the next level.

It took some doing, but I was able to secure them between all my rubber teeth. Shook my head a few times to make sure they didn't fly out. Even burrowed my face deeper into all that tall grass, cutting better than I expected.

I waited behind some trash cans at the side of the double-wide for the next group of trick-or-treaters to pass by. When they finally did, I only heard them coming because they were all talking so much shit about each other's costumes, kicking dirt and gravel up at each other with some fuck-you's thrown back and forth. The mummy wasn't wrapped up enough. The witch's hat was too short. Frankenstein didn't even have the bolts sticking out of her neck. They were a good twenty feet ahead of me when I tore out from behind the trash cans, growling, spitting inside my mask, nearly breaking my neck because I was shaking my wolf's head around so damn hard.

Easy target. I went straight for the mummy, tore the gauze to absolute shreds. Didn't cut him or anything, just left him only a couple ounces of his costume remaining before Frankenstein pulled me off of him, saying something in my ear like "Not yet, not yet." I kicked around in the air so the witch wouldn't come at me and that sort of broke me free from Frankenstein too. Next was the nearest trailer.

Empty porch except for one lonely Jack-o-Lantern and a birdhouse with moss growing on it that read "GOD BLESS." Still remember, it had a big smile of terribly carved sharp teeth. Rapped at the doorknocker all the way to hell, howling through my human teeth and everything. A friendly couple opened the door chuckling about how eager this kid was to get some candy. But I just threw my face into their bowl. The dad's face flashed across my mind, held up by his stupid fucking cape.

Shredded all the wrappers and all the chocolate inside. Got their knuckles too. I noticed it, the blood spraying onto the floor as they dropped the bowl. I heard them scream, but I didn't let myself think anything of it. I just ran out into the street howling.

My friends were at the end of the block. Their pillow cases were absolutely slammed with candy, just begging to be cut open. And was visualizing how I'd pull my mask off and laugh, they'd see it was me and punch me in the shoulder, maybe even the gut, and it'd all just be a hell of a prank. But there were too many others to pass up in the small stretch of dirt road between me and them.

I tore up a cardboard robot costume. Made a few parents shriek as I tried to gnaw at their dog leash. I shredded the cloak of a plastic reaper and left slashes across the name on a styrofoam gravestone. There was a lot of cackling and some of the older kids who were babysitting their little siblings cheered me on. So I was howling–from the absolute bottom of my stomach. That's when I caught up with my friends, but before I could latch on to one of their candy loads, one of them screamed out, "Netti! Fucking stop it!" They all sort of held their pillow cases back with a hand out in front of them to push me back if I came at them. The others I was able to see through the eye-holes in my mask seemed to be ignoring the standoff, probably happy that the wild kid was being dealt with by his peers. As distance between me and my friends was starting to feel more and more tangible, I crouched down, hopping side to side, growling, snarling. They asked me what the hell I was doing, why I had to be this way. But it was too late for answers. I was one with the unrisen moon.

I went mask-first into one of their arms, grabbed their wrist and elbow, and started shaking. All the sounds blurred together, but the smell of it was perfectly divided. Blood. Rubber. Rust. I can feel it stinging my sinuses now. Still burns when I think about it. Then, one of them clocked me. Knocked the hell out of the side of my head and I was on my ass. Someone ripped off my mask and asked me what the fuck was my problem.

My friend, Steph—I couldn't see her during my little escapade—was the one holding her arm, collapsed on the gravel with a big splatter of blood all around her. That's when I felt the cuts on my own face, ran my fingers along the lines; they went criss-crossed along my cheeks and mouth, deeper than I would have guessed they would go. I was aware of the pain for the first time and I started to wail right there in the middle of the road.

There were a few parents around who came over to see about all the blood on Steph's arm and the cuts on my face and what we were all screaming about. But I slapped their hands away. A pang of guilt lodged into me, not for Steph, or even for my own face. The expression of the dad in the cape loomed ahead. I felt awful for hating him off the bat like that. For thinking he must be some kind of backward asshole like I was that night.

And I was off. Fucking blood running down my shirt and I was still bawling, hauling ass again down the street. And you know how kids are— no way I was going home to tell my mom about what I did. Didn't have a plan; I was just running. Until I passed the double-wide with the shed.

I figured I could stay under the shed a while; it was completely dark and the grass looked white under the moon. No sign of the family inside either. It'd be a safe hideout for a few hours. And that's how long it felt like I was crawling through the yard. I was on my belly again, inching my way through in case the family came back at any time. But it's like the grass was getting thicker, and taller too. Until I could eventually stand up, completely hidden by the growth around me. And I must have been walking in circles or something because I was getting nowhere. And it started to set in—the feeling that I was lost. Bugs hopping down from the grass, landing in my mouth and in my ears. And it was right when the panic was starting to really show itself that I saw a slight path. Where someone else had walked through the yard before, the grass parted just slightly. And for all I know, it might have been my own trail. But I'm not so sure, considering where it led me.

I followed it to the shed, to the loose panel at the bottom of its construction. And, with how the night had gone so far, it felt familiar and safe. Like your favorite hiding spot as a little kid, where there's no fucking way anyone could find you. Like you're so hidden away that it's cheating. So I left the moonlight behind me and crawled inside.

It was cold by then, which was great news for me because the heat of the blood seemed to be burning its way across my face, neck, and chest. Stuck to my skin like it was just another layer I was born with, something they'd have to cut me out of so I could be like the rest of them. So, I just crawled real slow through the mud, letting it cool me off. And with each movement, I would sort of splay my fingers out. I was curious about what else I may find down there. And there wasn't a box. But I did grab a handful of cloth. It was heavy, like the dad's necromancer cape, but shredded. And it was weighted, tied to something heavy. So I inched forward, letting my hand feel its way up. Until my fingers got tangled in the hair. My face burned all over again. But, I kept feeling around, and the hair disappeared into the forehead. And then the nose and eyes. Then the mouth–all cut up to hell. Crisscrossed, deeper than you'd think. The remaining skin was loose, and cold, not enough left to snarl. Cut up into pieces, the face could have formed an infinite number of new shapes. And, I don't feel great about this next part, but it's what happened.

I laid there, moving the skin into new expressions and different looks. And there, in the lightless black of under the shed, I could hear myself smile. It hurt like hell.

INTERLUDE- SNAIL MEAT!

They sell escargot in the damndest of places. Before the second wave of disco, you could only buy it in heavily reviewed restaurants and in the backrooms of the clubs, the kind with sex workers the price of the 5-star menus. But as disco died, so did the meat buttered down into the shells. The tendons, that were just clinging to spirals, thrown down the sink, building masses at the pipe joints until it's all blasted away by drain cleaner.

But, with disco back in the city, escargot was revived in its succulence, full-bodied, filling its shell with the flavor of roasted butter. Sold in the back alleys, the ones that taste like blood and smell like a fuck on a smoke break. Priced by the half dozen for the same prices as they were before, kept warm in the bags of killed-off pizza delivery boys.

The cooks are what's important though. They're the kind who wouldn't stop staring in high school, measuring the triceps of the football players, the weight of mop-haired arrogant test-takers. They stared until school was over and, afterward, they were staring at the wall of their basement, waiting for it to slicken with lichens, the kind they'd loved, the only kind they'd focused on, rented texts from the library to learn its different mystic, scientific names. Tasting the lichens when no one was looking, and no one was ever looking in the basement. These were the best cooks, the ones who never gave a Mixing Boy trouble when they bought the flakes.

Like the lichens, they knew the flakes. The color, the flavor: bitter or melancholic—determined by the region of the city, taking in the effects of lights, movement, violence, the shape according to the various kinds of graters they would use against the demon flesh. The latest drug-addled innovation in Murder City

Anyone could throw flakes into their next meal. It was simple. But, the cooks knew how to arouse all its properties in the process. The butter and the seasoning were important, but more than anything it was the former life they paired it with. Flakes on powerful, lean meats, red all the way to the center, came on strong and ended with even more fury. Pairing with white meats worked their way up but never stimulated the body to any kind of elevated state. The trick was to find something weak, yet resilient. The way snails slide, so slowly across the slick concrete, trailing silver geometries behind them. Their bodies wilting under a few pinches of salt, but capable of eating a carcass a thousand times their size. Pair that with the oven-roasted, grated flesh of a Feather Demon. And the high will last for days. Slurp from the spiral in the alley and feel unreal by the time you make your way home.

If you take several shells at once, you'll be well enough to circle the city and spiral your way back to the place you're standing now—a cook staring at you in the alley just like he used to stare at the wall of his basement. He's taking note of your expression; you're so animalistically confident. The cook is blank, the sound of lichen growing. Making the miracle of his escargot the more unbelievable. You hate the feeling and leave him behind, the sound of shells crunching under your patent leather shoes. The cars all sludged together, the exhaust reduced to liquid, binding the windows shut. Everyone has the same face in every cab, van, truck, ill-intentioned sports car. It's the face of the cook.

And that's the high. Someone else's face wrapped around the city, wrapped so tight that it's staring right at you. That, even in the blankness of the stare, you're being observed. And as there are countless lichen eyes focused on you, there's a chance that the city isn't indifferent, that it might give you a spiral-shaped shell. You pass out in your own bed. And when you wake up, the bagel shop's neon sign buzzes in the morning dark across the street and the air is warm through your window. Your tongue, it tastes like snail meat.

IT HURTS LIKE A MOTHER-FUCKER

It's brightly lit in the bagel shop. The warm grain in the air is something like a fur coat when Netti walks in with the detective. A woman with the hair of an artfully deconstructed beehive waves them down. Leaning over to the detective, he explains this is Vega from the marketing team.

"Detective," Vega reaches out a hand, "It's so nice to meet you."

Castra returns the greeting and they sit down. Netti pulls up a chair from another table, facing the window. The afternoon crowd ambles down the sidewalk outside—high-waisted pants and leisure suits in the last heat of the year.

"That's what Netti was telling me," Castra goes on, not thinking much of his absence of attention.

He forces his focus a minute or two and learns the marketer's name is Vega. And Castra's being a real sweetheart.

Vega's charming, "So, you must stay pretty busy with your work?"

"I stay as busy as anyone else."

"Now, Detective Castra, I love this city as much as the next girl. But, I'm not blind to the fact that a detective wouldn't be pushed beyond her mortal limits in a place like this."

"Since you put it like that…"

"No, no. I mean that as a compliment to you. I used to dream of doing what you do, but I was always terrible at logic. Barely passed Intro to Philosophy last semester, and it was pretty embarrassing."

"I can see your grades in the way you hold your spine. You're tense, kid. Should check out one of those needle places. Loosen you right up. But, anyway, who were you studying?" Castra asks.

Vega, thinks for a second, as if wondering what parts of Castra's reply to ignore, "I don't remember the names. Like I said, I was much, much better at my marketing classes, art history too. But, I mainly remember one man, talking something about an image that looked like a rabbit and a duck all at once. I don't know. His dad was a tycoon and his brother played piano. But he lost his hand in the war. So, when he got home, he had to learn to play one-handed. Still performed, sold tickets to his concerts. Wish I could've seen it."

"Sounds like he would have fit right in here."

"You've lived here your whole life?" asks Vega.

"Actually, no. I took a job here shortly after I started my career in criminal justice. My hometown was the type of place with more birds on the telephone wires than people on the streets. The sidewalks stayed clean because every shop owner went out after a thunderstorm to brush away all the loose branches and soaked pieces of trash."

But Netti's looking out the window. He sees a Pretty Face's mask the color of heat ambling along the gutter. He's seen it before, several times, but was never able to make the grab. Winks at Castra, but she doesn't think one thing or another that he leaves the table with a theatrical cough. A little nod in his direction, like a customer saying goodbye to the apron behind the cash register.

Vega sees his fur coat waving through the street for a second before he's gone in the crowd, laughs a little as she notes every sound coming out of the detective's mouth.

"He's an artist-type. Can't be trusted," Castra jokes.

"I think his style's perfect."

"I get enough of him in my 9-5. So, tell me, Vega. What do you have going on?"

Vega pulls out a crisp notebook, "The agency I'm interning at, we've been going out into the city. Me, not as much, because of my other classes. But, Netti's a friend of ours, as you know, Detective, and he said you'd be a great person to meet."

"And what are you doing when you meet these people?"

"Right, sorry," Vega's already taking notes, "We're interviewing them," her tone breaks into something practiced, "First, and more than anything, to get to know the city that we enjoy, and just happen to be promoting. And, also to tell the story of its people. If this story-telling goes well, it'll land in the newspapers; we're working on some billboard campaigns so I could see something like this being featured in that venue. And, it's not where we started as an agency, but we are looking to break into radio ads, which is what I'm most excited about."

"What do you want to know about me?" Castra asks. "About the city?"

"We'll, that's the heart of it right there. You are the city, aren't you?" Vega scrawls a line across her notepad, "Wasn't going to lead with that obviously. I usually try to lead the conversation where I think the meaning is."

"That won't last you long."

"My interviewing process?" Vega asks.

"Your search for meaning. Or, less of a search. More of an expectation that it's there at the end waiting for you."

"You really don't believe there is any meaning in all of this?"

"Nothing that grim," Castra answers. "There are… moments. So full of meaning that it hurts like a motherfucker, time blocks so heavy there's no way you could move them, or move your way around it in the end. That's where the meaning is."

"Is that what you do in your work then? Find the dark moments or… time blocks? And what do you do once you find one?"

"Would an example help?"

Vega says yes.

Castra tells the story, "I moved here during the first disco wave, just before the dead bird cycle. It was a beautiful time. I'd just finished my work in the academy and I felt stronger than ever. I could go into an interrogation room with the same confidence as a dance floor. I was young and it was like the skin on my knuckles could never break. For a while, I was tougher than those tough times. It was all over me. People wanted to fuck with me to see if I would break. One night, there was a dealer who was giving out disco biscuits for free. He wanted to see what would happen if the circle around him thought they could fly.

So a handful of us took a good dose, nothing wild. Just enough. Once the effects started to kick in around our table in the back corner, a few of us were crying. Classic symptoms. Slurring our regrets and the others caught what we had to say and spun it into silver linings. One of us had killed their childhood cat the day they got their license. One of us had set fire to a letter from their grandparents, never opened, waved it around the bonfire at summer camp in front of all the other scouts. One of us had crushed flowers into a blood-red paste and painted it across the door of their house and their sister went missing the next week. Another one found his dad's cut-up body under a shed and didn't say shit to anyone about it. The table we sat around was a vortex. Nothing could leave it, none of what we confessed. None of what they tried to twist into… meaning.

Like always, we all came down. The sun was rising and it was time to find our separate ways home. Naturally, I followed the dealer. The morning was humid. I could have bit the air in half. I was faster than him, one hundred feet behind and covering all the ground between us.

By the time I caught up to him, he was taking a piss in an alleyway. When he zipped up and turned around, I had my gun under his throat. The way the barrel of the pistol sunk into his skin showed all the acne scars that had been doing their best to heal over the last twenty years.

His breaths were short and careful, moving the gun metal with each one. Made me stick up his chin even harder. It was tough for him to talk, but they always find a way.

He asked what I wanted.

I pointed out that he didn't confess to anything. And I asked if he thought that was fair. Pointed the gun directly down his ear to give him a second to breathe.

He agreed—it wasn't fair. And, Vega," Castra wraps her fingers around the kid's hand. "It was storytime, motherfucker.

Something about how he used to love going to a car wash. It was his favorite thing to do between classes his last year of high school when his schedule was wide open. He had nothing but time and an ashtray of quarters, it seems.

The more school went on, the more he skipped, and the more he visited the car wash. Slowly, it started to lose its magic. And, somehow his life had gotten to the point where the logical next step was to send an empty car down the tunnel of spinning brushes and foam.

It was also the year that all the dead birds were appearing in parking lots. So he spent the greater part of a morning collecting them, stacking them up in the front and back seats of his car. There were feather barbs under his fingernails by the time he was done. He drove up, nestled against all the dead birds, and bolted as soon as his car hit the belt to take it down the tunnel. Ran all the way around the back to hide in the bushes for a view of what was to come.

It was the owner of the carwash who came out first. Visored his fingers against his face to peek inside the immaculately cleaned car exterior. He sighed. Only a father can breathe with that sort of resignation. Went inside, dialed a few numbers, waved his shaking hands in the air with uncertainty as he surely didn't have the words to communicate this kind of stress.

But, he got to work. Rolled up his sleeves, placed his glasses in his shirt pocket, and reached in to shift the car into neutral. Rolled it into the shade while all his other customers made their way sparkling out of the parking lot. He began to make a pile.

He didn't know it at the time, but he started with the dry birds. Dropped brown ones on top of red ones and black ones on top of blue ones. The breeze began to blow and small feathers began to drift into the car wash tunnel. So small that they were only visible if you watched it leave the body of the bird and swirl all the way into the point of vanishing as it entered the cleaning barrage. Next, were the wet ones. The kid had cracked the back right window just enough for some water and suds to find their way inside the car and make a thin puddle around the larks stacked carefully on the backseat. And he watched as the man stacked the slick bodies in a small pyramid under the tree.

That was it. All he needed to confess. A few months later, I shot him in a drug raid, right under his jaw."

Vega's written pages of notes, illustrations even. She takes a shallow breath, straightens her shoulder like the women she saw in the ads, telling the wonders of multi-purpose kitchen tools, stainless steel blades pointing in every direction.

INTERMISSION – THE DELI GROWS UNBEARABLE!

The demons have been in the city for some time now, and business at the Discoteque is good. Taran Adderly even has a date. They eat at a salad bar that night, a first outing that hasn't gone terribly. He's sure to compliment her dress one last time and ask if he might be able to take her out again. She says yes and falls asleep smiling at the ceiling, not even a demon at the foot of her bed. The next morning at the diner, he leaves an extra dime with his usual tip next to the last dregs of his coffee. And by the time he clocks out of work, he's secured a billboard partnership for his ad agency, just in time to bump up his quarterly bonus.

He squares away some wire transfers and drops into a bagel shop for something that could soak up his nerves. The Asiago whole-grain heats his face with each bite. The sidewalk is full of colder faces and he's starting to get his stride into something more confident. He'd picked the Disco with the lit-up tiles like he saw in that one movie and they would have something to look at if she didn't want to dance. Taran would dance regardless, a song or two to get it out of his system at the very least.

They nod to each other on the sidewalk outside the club. Taran covers her tip, brags to the doorman that her name is Gizelle and isn't that so damn beautiful? Bold enough now, he takes her hand and pulls her into the dark door. The corridor is smaller than anyone would think from the outside. It's tight like the off-shot arm of a deep cave, until it opens up all red. The whole room is one maroon. Taran points to the blue and purple light tiles, and as he smiles his teeth are all red too. Gizelle seems impressed. She matches step with Taran and they move lithely across the fringes of the dance floor. Not much movement under the lights yet. They'd have to start with drinks.

Bubbles swirl around ice in a collision of purple carbonation with the burn of two parts alcohol. Taran holds it up to his eyes, watches the crowd drift nervously along the walls, around the cocktail tables under their elbows, stray couples walking the in-between space of the bar and the rest of the club. Gizelle takes a vodka neat. And then another quickly after.

"Are you going to actually drink that?" Gizelle's eyes a little glazed. "Or are you just going to stare at it?'

"Don't be like that," he smiles, eyes still hidden behind the purple drink.

"I'm not. I'm genuinely curious. This city's full of people who just stare at their drinks. Have you noticed? I'm not joking."

"Well, in that case. Yes, but I like to let all the ice melt first, and wait until the bubbles are done. And, no. I don't really keep up with this city."

"I like drinks at their natural temperature."

"The temperature of the room."

"It's stasis. The closest we come to being in the womb on this side."

"That's unreal."

"You have no idea," she stares at the dance floor, a handful of couples beginning to move in vague zodiac shapes.

"How've you been? Since I saw you last."

"It was a long week," Gizelle's still staring. "Work's difficult these days."

"I couldn't do what you do."

"The last year has certainly brought in a new layer of nuance."

"Sounds fucking awful."

"I enjoy it," she drinks.

"Even when it's difficult?"

"I'd like to dance now," she finishes her third.

And when they reach the center of the floor, their bodies make curved lines in opposite directions as they turn. The edge of his jacket brushes the edge of her dress. Their wrists bend to the beat. The floor stays silent under the turning of their shoes and platforms. Her hair tangles into his. There's a man in a blue suit, twirling darkly in their shared periphery. An explosion of red-tinted white suits and dresses ruffle around him. The DJ has his hands raised to the ceiling like one might imagine God reaching toward the light above his head. Their hair has sweated into one mass gelled together.

By the end of the night, Taran secures another date, this one Gizelle's idea. She insists they go back to the same club. Taran agrees as a man in a fur coat bumps past him at the exit, his gaze on something in the distance. Taran's own eyes are glazed over with the dim light of the streets and the fluorescent orange of the solitary bulb screwed to the ceiling of her building's stoop casts a thin shadow over his face. Another date to the club would be nice.

Taran lies with his face slackened and void of any expression except for several hours' worth of sleep. The rest that's befallen him is so heavy in its darkness and dampness. The waking feels unnatural, the violent switching of opposite states. The first thing he's aware of is the static of the radio, the dial somehow having drifted clockwise while he was out, trading talk of pre-season injuries and an upside down economy for something like pure noise. The far corner of his mattress depresses with the weight of a visitor sitting down.

He's got a lonely slouch, straightening a little now. Taran's eyes move to the demon's suit. The floral print complements the faded paisley of his blankets, somehow, perfectly. The dancer in blue from the Disco. Or an imitation of the dancer in blue. It's always hard to tell with the way they slip in and out of their plane.

He knows this city, that he'd get paralyzed eventually. So he waits for the demon to notice he's awake, or waking. The visitor continues his tracing of the ceiling, rotating his shoulders to get the full scope of the room's four corners. Taran's watching the suit. The print of the fabric moving in a way that, to a man locked in sleep paralysis, means something. It's vibrant, seething with hermetic symbolism. It's paisley. It's high sorcery. The demon's feathers for eyes quiver, like a little wind is blowing across them, between the sleeper and the visitor.

Taran knows eye contact is inevitable. He knows he wants to see the feathers move in their sockets, having only heard the random corners of passing conversations about the phenomenon. He knows he wants to see them himself. But the demon's still reading his ceiling. Taran doesn't even try to move. That would be useless. His vocal cords have a shot though. He thinks of the feathers moving, visualizes his vocal cords doing the same, vibrating, sending something to make the demon turn his head. To look at him. The cords remain taught, pointed straight toward his brain, straight down his spine. Nothing.

But he can breathe. He exhales sharply against the top of his throat. It's almost shrill, but the demon is clearly lost in thought. It must be the pace of his breathing. He slows it down, out of the rhythm he'd been sleeping in but still nothing. The Feather Demon stares at nothing, not noticing the victim of his haunting, or possession, visitation. Taran focuses his attention deep inside of himself. He thrusts that focus upward and chokes it with the closing of his throat. A strange growl makes it past his teeth.

The friction of the sound loosens something in his chest, and his limbs quickly after. He throws his arms up in ecstasy, in being able to move. The demon is concerned. He throws himself across the bed and kneels over Taran's body. Long demon fingers lock on top of his sternum. Elbows crack into place. Then dead chest compressions. An inch at a time, the demon arms sink into his chest and rise back up again. Air flies in and out of Taran's body which has been reduced back to complete paralysis. His throat gurgles against the demon's presence, the sound climbs its way out of Taran's mouth only to slip back inside again and pounds at the insides of his cheeks. Only thin tendrils of spit make it out from between his lips, clinging to the skin of his face.

The chest compressions continue. Taran's ribs sink and rise until the demon gives up at sunrise, leaving his house behind, with the countenance of a forlorn doctor on a failed house call.

On the other side of downtown, Gizelle takes a trip to the bottom of her building, entering a restaurant nestled in its corner and taking an order of steaming noodles to go. Soon, she's passed out in the center of her king-size bed, a thin layer of broth, now cold, coating the styrofoam bowl on her nightstand. The sounds of the city outside her window are faint, the light pressure of brakes at stop signs, the hum of neon signs that stay on through the night. The city has its own paralysis.

The second date goes less well. Taran takes Gizelle back to the same Disco. She takes a drink before setting out to dance, but he's already left her for an empty space on the floor. He's moving with abandon at sharp angles, his feet planted to the purple and yellow flashing beneath his shoes. Other solo dancers drift his way, but he turns his back each time, glancing a look at Gizelle over his shoulder to make sure his date is still around. She sips her drink, a look of genuine concern coloring her brow. Taran's crying tears on the dance floor. He wipes them from his face as a queen with high-angled brows painted up her forehead pats him on the back. He tries to lift his feet, but the pain is too much to pick them up. He can't keep standing there. He flails his arms in a wave, totally divergent from the rest of the music. It's either a plea for help or a statement of resignation. The queen locks eyes with Gizelle and nods to tell her that it's okay. Gizelle pays the tab herself and leaves the club.

It's raining. The exit's understated. Splashes her way toward the nearest subway station, only three or four blocks away, less if you take the alleyways. But she doesn't. Gizelle takes off her shoes, lets her feet adjust to the temperature of the slick sidewalk–much colder than room temperature. The gutter is filthy with floating trash, swollen brochures about the city of demons: where to sleep at night, where to eat during the day. She's light on her feet in the rain and already halfway there. But there's a feeling rising within her that she's exhausted beyond catching up. That a night or week of sleep couldn't boot out the aching that's wriggling around behind her eyes. With a few blinks, she pushes the feeling down. It resides in her chest now. And her metro card is still good for a few more rides, she's pleased to find.

The bench is purple and yellow. The fluorescents above it make everything sterile. She slouches against the backrest, a heavy speed running perpendicular to her spine. There's no one else around at this hour but the window on the other side of the subway car flashes with variations of dark concrete and hissing pipes. The lights flicker, almost impersonally, with each bump and there are many bumps. The gnawing feeling of sleep crawls its way up from her chest, nestling itself back inside her head. And her eyes shut instinctually to lock it in.

When she wakes up paralyzed, she sees one sitting across from her. He doesn't notice her though, his eyes blue with feathers.

They're damp, dark. Rotating quietly on an axis in his sockets. They expand and condense into themselves, shades of black and purple showing themselves with the shifting of the movement. No direction to his gaze.

Only the peripheral arcs of his face moving right to left across the ceiling of the train car.

There's something about their visit that calms Gizelle. There's rest in her paralysis. Her demon is almost beautiful. It's not his appearance, only the way he observes his surroundings and what that must mean. If she could move, she might move closer. The feathers of his eyes gesture inward, even as they look outward. There's something familiar about the way she can't move. Motionless as the tunnel blurs by on the other side of the window.

It could be the graffiti. Thick marker curved and breaking into sharp directions to form something illegible. But a demon wouldn't know that, she thinks. Her visitor must think the lines make some kind of sense of the space they're sharing.

It's their third date and both of them start the night with heavy eyes. The same Disco club, the same set of drinks. And everything about every movement of theirs seems to shrug about the fact that they'll fuck later that night. Their drinks feel heavy in their hands, tasting like iron, swishing over their molars. They don't finish what's in front of them. The floor only partially crowded. They dance. Aware of every time a limb swivels on its joint. Aware of each time they rise off of or slide across the floor. The DJ drops record after record under the needle. But tonight is one for the extended cuts, each album spinning out at lengths of time that would make any sober person furious.

The white dresses, the white jackets, the man in the fur coat, all around her move a little slower than they did when they first started dancing. One of them raises his shoulder to his face, absorbing a tear in his jacket, disguising the motion as dance. There's a woman on the other side of her with her hand covering her eyes in shame, feet still moving to the rhythm. There's nothing to be had at this club. They leave in a slow flashing of purple and burgundy lights.

The sandwich shop is hotter than usual on the night they both die. Gizelle wipes off her makeup at the table, drops the napkin beside her plate. Taran keeps asking her if she wants to try his Marbled Rye Reuben. She's enjoying the Philly Cheese just fine.

"Are you sure? It looks-" he grimaces. "Revolting."

"Gizelle raises the enormous sandwich effortlessly to her face. Steam drifts from the grilled peppers spilling from its sides.

Taran wonders how any food could stay so hot for so long.

She smiles, wondering the same thing.

"How's yours?"

He's eaten half of his Reuben, carefully, in the pattern of the marbling of the bread, following the curves with each successive bite.

Other couples from the Disco walk by the deli, some passing on into the streets and others entering their own order of sandwiches. It's typical of the witching hour, for dates to leave the club and place things in their stomachs, only to return for more dancing at a less liminal hour. Taran and Gizelle discuss whose apartment they should go to after this. The conversation is transactional, starting to be drowned out by the sound of the line at the front counter, men ordering Cubans, women taking the Ham on Rye. Each couple eventually takes a seat as they wait for their order to come out. And each couple is replaced by another one at the line. The deli begins to run out of space dind the sandwiches that come out of the kitchen to the tables seem to be more absurdly large than the last time. Even more couples enter the deli. And by the time Gizelle and Taran decide that they'll go back to her place, it's become apparent that they won't be able to squeeze their way out for some time.

Drops of conversations come together in the space between the club-goers and the ceiling of the deli, rippling upward, splashing like a disturbing heel has landed directly in the middle of it all. The noise so loud that Taran and Gizelle lower their faces to the table, heads pressed together so they can hear each other speak. They talk for an hour more. They grow tired. Their words drift into a realm of meaning that, somehow, makes sense of the bodies in motion behind them, the ones they can't see, but feel bustling against them. But they could never understand the extent while fully awake. Soon, two of the bodies surrounding them are their paralysis demons.

They're uncomfortable, these Feather Demons, in the crowd. Torsos body into theirs and the movement sends a stiffness all through their countenance. Feathers begin to fall from their eye sockets. Just one or two at first. Floating side to side in a swing motion around the shuffling of knees and shoes. More come down, straighter now in their fall. Sticking to the floor. Something dark and wet melding them to the tiles. A molted pile of drenched feathers. The demons try to stop it. They hold their hands over their eyes. But the feathers seep out from between their fingers. It's getting worse. Feathers that might as well be bodily fluid.

Something must be done. But their visitees are asleep, paralyzed. The demons hesitate with their hands still tensed against their eyes, getting shoved unintentionally from the crowd around them. Then, they let go. Feathers land with full gravity in fistfuls of clumps on the floor, the table, Taran and Gizelle. They throw their long fingers around the shoulders of their couple and shake them outrageously, ready for them to wake up. To have the couple's conscious mind acknowledge them, send them some-where else where there are less people and pain.

The shaking isn't working. They increase the roughness, slightly. The sound of the crowd in the deli grows unbearable. But, with time, the shaking grows violent, slinging their heads and necks around at all angles, not waking them up, but still shaking them until there's a distinct crack, and then a second one, that pops through the building. A boy at the slicer in the back hears the vertebrae crack off of one another. A man in a fur coat walks by the deli on the sidewalk. He wonders if this is gonna be the shame, the death of these two strangers, that makes him feel again. He has a feeling it won't.

GRIMOIRE RADIO – CALL #2

"Welcome to another segment of Grimoire Radio. That was the fucking Bee Gees. I'm DJ Calling Card and we're taking a moment to pick up the needle and hear from our listeners about their experience with the ever so present, ever so slick, sleep paralysis demons of Murder City.

And, I've got a live one on the line right here, right now.

Beloved listener, what is your name?"

"Steph."

"And are you a long time listener of the show, Steph?"

"Since the beginning."

"Well, that brings me whole airwaves of joy to hear. I hope you can hear the gratitude in my voice. Now, tell me. What kind of demon are we talking today? Feathers? Pretty Faces? And you know we're always eager for a good Whisper Tooth story. Those are," he lets his faceless voice trail off into the darkness, "so few and far between."

"This is a story about a Pretty Face and me."

"Well, we're gonna take what we can get, right? Never been disappointed by a caller's story anyway. Go on now. Tell us your Pretty Face story. Would you," he takes a stylish pause, "Begin with the mask it wore? When it visited you that night?"

"It was like a pig. But no eyes or ears, only a big snout covering the whole face. Two tusks, the ones that curve back toward the face of wild pigs. This one was poorly made though. Paper mache and globs of paint. It was still wet too. Barely holding itself together. I wanted so badly to take a handful of all that wet paper and tear it away from that empty face.

But, obviously, I was paralyzed. And that wouldn't have been a problem if I was by myself. But my roommate was knocked out in bed on the other side of the room."

I watched the Pretty Face step off my mattress and walk toward my roommates' bed. And I hadn't noticed this until that point but it was carrying something behind its back.

You know those bolt guns–the ones used to kill farm animals? You put the little cartridge in them and pull the trigger, then the bolt punches through the skull between the eyes. Slides in and out of the animal's brain faster than you can see it. It just drops them. They don't feel a thing, I don't think.

Well, the worst part was maybe when I saw my roommate wake up. His eyes opened so slow. Like his eyelids were grating his retinas. Even in the dark, I could see his pupils expand to take in the whole sight of the demon. But, the demon was already kneeling over his chest, knees on his arms, pinning him to the bed.

He was able to look at me. I was paralyzed, unable to do anything.

It pulled the bolt gun from around its back. Opened a chamber with long, seemingly weak fingers. Then reached those same fingers up into its pig snout. Pulled out something shining. For a second, it was the only thing you could see in the room. An angry glimmer.

Then I saw my roommate's fingers. John. His name was John. I saw his fingers and his hands and his forearms waving around in the air. Trying to get the demon off him. Throwing his face from side to side as it lowers the bolt gun to his howling expression.

The barrel touched him between the eyes more than once, but John thrashed away each time. That's when the demon just starts poking the gun at his face. Striking wherever he is at the moment. Just the barrel at first, leaving circles and crescents of blood where the metal opened the skin. Then it pulls the trigger.

It sounds like someone sucking in air. Then a crunch, little but dense. The bolt's broken all his front teeth in half. But he's still resisting. Blood and spit just roping out of his mouth as he squirms around under the gun.

The demon digs its fingers into the snout again, pulls out another cartridge. Slips it into the gun like it's getting more steady as time goes on. I think John was wearing out when it pulled the trigger a second time. Another crunch but this time more wet. Caved his eye socket in.

John didn't have a lot left after that. Moving around more out of pain than fight. And, you know the way these things go. The shock of the second crunch set my arms free a little and I was able to throw my body out of my bed to at least try to go help. But the third crunch came the second I hit the floor."

"Well, oh my good god, that's gonna be the way we end Grimoire Radio today. Thank you for calling, Steph. It's listeners like you that make Grimoire Radio what it is. And to the rest of you, don't hesitate to ring our phones off the hook. Hit us with whatever you've got, but you all know by now that we're just hungry for some Whisper Teeth Demon encounters. Now, here's Abba!"

WHAT'S IN THE GUTTERS

Today, Netti works slowly. It hurts whenever it happens. He looks around at the others, taking their stacks to the inkers across the hall–still trying to get the wolf to poke his snout above the boil surface of a jacuzzi, staking out an emissary's lurid love affair. It really shouldn't be as difficult as he's found it to be. A simple appearance of nostrils, expanding for an inhale of steam, an exhale, a disappearance of the snout. But the work is fucking slow. The lines go down on the paper too thick, the angles too soft, the shading too dense. He notices an insecurity in himself, drifting, that's new. He worries the detective will notice when she stops by. The Mixing Boys already must be wondering why he hasn't come over today. He even invited the marketing team, taking them up on their offer to do a city spotlight on him.

Only just this morning, he'd spun at the thought of them all meeting. To see his sketches, his skill–both an afterthought to the mask he'd stolen last night.

And, to write a profile on both Castra and him, working together, the things it would say on what it means to be a detective. What does time mean to violence? What is mystery in relation to space? He starts to sweat under his coat as he begins to shade in the gentle boil of the jacuzzi's surface.

A story gnaws its way into his focus, but he tries to blur the edges, attempts to just breathe in the graphite, the only physicality of one of his few skills in life. But the abstraction of the story is too heavy, marble-like, bulging through a thin membrane of gray matter made weak by years of early drug abuse. Until it breaks, in a hot flood of liquid memories that make themselves known with the ghost of an acidic taste conjuring itself on the back of Netti's tongue.

He thinks of his neighbor, Steph, and all the movie nights they began with their makeshift rituals. The older they became, the later they stayed up, and the more their movies splattered themselves in the square of the television with flesh-colored stretches and melts. Sacred, at first, they grew numb to the primal fears of watching one of their peers take a barrage of stabbings to the torso. But, then a new thing settled in them. Once their minds' guts began to grasp that these were practical effects and that the acting was shit, it was the cheapness of it that began to create a feeling of unease. Knowing that someone, in earnest, was fighting for their big break with their contrived final breaths before the killer revealed themself to the victim. The speed of the camera as it zoomed in on the violence, the effort of the Director and cinematographer on graphic display.

"Netti, honey. You've got a visitor!"

One of the Mixing Boys waves jazz hands splattered in monster green, accentuating the presence of Vega, hunched over her notebook.

Netti looks at her eyes, trying to place her, and her role on the team.

She looks back, knowing he doesn't recognize her, though he's trying. It grimaces across his face as he forces a smile.

"Netti! Don't you remember Vega? She's practically the co-captain at the only marketing agency who has the balls to stay in town."

Vega straightens up a bit, "I'm just the copywriter. Getting college credit and everything for this. But, in a way you could say I'm running things," she laughs, just a little, "Yeah, you'd be surprised with what I can convince them to let me do."

The Mixing Boy shakes her by the shoulders, "This is what I'm fucking talking about... A captain!"

Netti realizes he hasn't walked over to his guest yet, crosses the room still holding his pencil, "You might have come to interview me, but–and it doesn't seem like I'm alone here–I want to hear more about all this steering of the ship."

He thinks of Steph, of the time they carved a pentagram into the faux wood panel of their television set to keep themselves safe. Ritual. That was going to be his angle for this story. Detective work as ritual.

"—so I sent it to the printer anyway. Meaning we'll see a no-punches piece on Castra's insanity."

Netti tucks his pencil into his pocket, "Well, don't get too hot and bothered about it right now, Vega," he starts to whisper, "She'll be here any minute now."

The Mixing Boy cuts in, "Yeah, I heard about that. The Director actually said we should host her in the basement."

Netti, with style, gnaws at a fingernail with his glistening teeth, "Really? That doesn't seem…"

"I'm down for wherever," Vega assures them.

"That doesn't seem," Netti continues, "Like the most hospitable spot in the building."

"It's what she said. Come on, she's probably already down there by now."

"That sounds great," Vega jumps ahead, somehow knowing the way to the basement.

"Netti," the Mixing Boy grabs fistfuls of the inbetweener's hair, "It's going to be alright. We've thought about this."

The basement is immaculately furnished. Persian rugs, a mixture of imitation and originals, thicken the floor. And the walls have a few new landscape paintings–the subject of which is buried deep in the background with near invisible brush strokes–with noxiously swirling gilt gold frames. There's even a light fixture, hanging down where the spinning wheel of Feather Demons was just a few days, perhaps weeks, ago when Netti was allowed to visit for the first time. The Director and Detective Castra are sharing a hookah, passing the pipe with each turn of the conversation and sharing a big single cloud of smoke the color of gray organs just after they're cut from a body.

"And you remember the Workhorse Quartet, don't you?" the Director asks.

"Oh, I came to the city right after their time. That's my understanding anyway."

"So you didn't grow up here? I would have sworn."

"No, I moved in for the job. Was able to join as detective right off the bat, so I was lucky enough to just come right in," says Castra.

"Oh, you little cunt. That's a bunch of fucking bullshit."

Castra responds, "I wouldn't take you for the type to disbelieve a woman moving up in her profession."

"The detective bit, I believe. It's in your bone structure. Obvious. What I don't believe is the fact that you came to this city for a job."

"I'm not sure what to tell you. Moved here because I got a job. The job was here. In the city."

"Oh, that's brilliant," the Director says. "Really figured out where your own job is. That's some sexy detective work if I've ever witnessed it. No, Castra. If you chose this city, then there has to be something deeper, something about you that gets it. And I know you get it. That's written all over your face, the enjoyment you take in all of this. The comfort you experience here. You know other places, other people, aren't like us. It's almost like there's a smell in the air. Like our world has fucked another world and given birth to another all at the same time. And, if you're the right kind of person, the kind of person who would find themselves drawn to this coital little city, you might find that exciting. So, detective, what is it that brings you to this city?"

"Well," Castra's happy to be caught, "since you asked, and I'm not sure

I've ever said this out loud. Certainly not on the clock. It's the gutters."

"The. Gutters. I love that."

Castra goes on, "But, it's more about what's in the gutters. The rain stays there for absurd amounts of time. I'm not sure if other cities have more hills or inclines and we're just stacking our buildings on top of a flat plane. But it's like the water pools up inside of them and then never leaves. The way a family of mice will cut through the puddle in a trail of little bodies. And underneath their feet, you know the water is just teeming with shitty little bacteria. Microscopic organisms eating each other with their invisible jaws. Amoebas splitting themselves into two. And we just step on it. All that grimy violence just ended with nothing but a commuter stepping onto the bus. Our very being here is a violence. All we have to do is move and we find ourselves killing."

"Oh my god, Castra. I'm in love. With your words, you, all the amoebas who split themselves in two—I just want to scoop them up in my hand and feed them mouse guts with my fingertips. It's just so fucking gorgeous, detective. I'm so glad you've come to our city."

"But, we haven't spoken about you. You talk like someone who was raised here," Castra replies.

"Not at all."

"Well?"

The Director gets around to it, "Like you, I chose to come here. But it wasn't the gutters in the street. To be perfectly frank, I don't relish the idea of telling this to a woman of the law but to be perfectly honest it's the drugs."

She's been waiting for this, beams in a way that begs to tell her more.

"And it's not what you think. Not the disco biscuits, not even Feathers. It's those little purple sleeping pills. Well, they're gone now. The kids move on. But, while they were here, they were by far the most over-the-counter method for ODing your way into sleepwalking out some cruelty that was just beyond your reach in the waking hours. And if I were to get introspective about it, I'd probably say that trying to rediscover that feeling is part of why I do what I do for work. Getting to direct lucid descents into brutishness." She motions to the space all around her, "is the reason I make this cartoon. It's the reason behind every suspect, and every bloody puzzle that the wolf has to piece together with nothing but his paws and whatever we draw inside of his coat pockets. It's cruel as shit; I can't get enough of it! So here we are, every fucking week–a new void to hurl our little fiction into, and he just has to claw his way out. But, damn it, he does it. He does it every goddamn week. We all do. Somehow. We don't even like it half the time. But we all fuck our way out by the end. That's the dream we keep dreaming every single night, the sleeping pills we chew up with our bourbon at the bedside table–taking a whole handful in hopes it might send us out the window in our sleep this time."

Netti wants to burn a line of cocaine through his nostrils. He shakes his head until the feeling starts to be replaced by another. He wants to cover his face. To breathe through a layer of thread that only a demon could weave together. He wants to climb over a demon in its ritual succubus act of draining and take that mask in the first place. He wants to fucking consume Murder City.

Detective Castra doesn't look much different. Though her face is perfectly relaxed, her eyes are protruding just slightly with the need for cruelty. She catches herself, "I think I know what you mean, Director. And I hate to say it, but I have to get to work. I hope we can do this again sometime. I'm eager to hear more about your job. You described it so vividly, but I still feel like I'm only looking at it diagonally. But, that's obvious, we both know what happens. No need to hide that. But, I'm still over here doing my best detective work trying to figure out what else you might be talking about. Other than the Feathers, the cartoons, and whatever the hell you've been doing with Netti. But, like I said, if you'd have me, I'd come back.

Something tells me you'd welcome that sort of thing."

Netti's turned green, glances out of the corner of his eye to see if Vega is still taking notes. She won't stop. None of this will ever stop.

INTERLUDE – WHAT'S ON THE MENU!

OK, the menu you presented to me is a great start. It's sexy and it's beautiful and the dishes alone are dripping with decadence. All of those are beautiful things. However, I wanna push you just a step further and get you thinking from the perspective of a tourist. If people are traveling to this city, and they want the full experience of this city every step of the way. Just think about it. Anyone who goes to the Northland Park, wants little rabbit ears cut into their sandwiches and on their hats as they leave for the parking lot. We have to do that same thing for your steakhouse. But for demons. Now, I will say that I'm not proposing a shift in your offerings, not at all. Like I said, I think these are perfect. What I am proposing is a shift in presentation and perspective.

So this… Is what I'm proposing.

And to really draw the point home, something I have to do with all my clients, and it may feel a little weird at first, but I like to write out a story. A story of the ideal diner at your restaurant having the best goddamn night of their lives.

Two men. Not brothers. But lovers. They've come from the north to see Murder City. When they arrive they asked around the kiosks at the station for an authentic experience.

See, there are reparations to be made. There's been unfaithfulness in the relationship and an enormous slab of dissatisfaction in the bedroom. The weight of their own feelings has pulverized other areas of their life as well. Their work. Their friends. Their conversations with their nieces and their nephews about their college classes. They just need to feel something. See, it took them years to get together. Knew each other as kids but couldn't stomach the acknowledgement until years later, when the first wrinkles began creasing around their eyes. So they make their way to Murder City! Once they're here, and they know the right steakhouse to visit because of our current sponsors on the kiosks, they smile a little learnedly as the waiter lights a candle between them and drops down a menu. When it hits the table it's clear that it has the heft of a weapon for up close and personal violence.

They share a chuckle over the titles and exclaim that Oh this is just perfect. They ask if the other noticed the caviar, or the house salad. There is an attentiveness between them that hasn't been sparked in some time. The menu alone is reigniting something in their marriage.

When their waitress returns, each places an order for red wine and one order of Oyster Death, and Disco Tartare as well.

Waiting, they ask if the other is rested up from their nap after the trip. They both were surprised by the amount of energy they have. Their body language is inquiring of each other from across the table. There are questions. There are unvoiced questions about what will happen after dinner once they get back to the room. It's a long while, nearly one whole glass of slowly sipped wine, before they realize they've been moving to the beat of a chopping knife in the kitchen and knife chopping to the rhythm of a disco single, the club mix extended to eight minutes of revelry. When the waiter comes back with their second glass, they ask him for the name of this song. He gives a practiced shrug and a smiling reply that it's just whatever the disco is playing, that there is a heavy cable running from a speaker in the kitchen out through the plumbing and under two blocks of downtown connected to the PA system of the club. So, while enjoying the best steak dinner of their lives, they're also getting a live take on the dance floor hysterics.

They look at each other with a Wow-can-you-believe-this-shrug-of-the-shoulders. That's when the food comes out. The tartare couldn't be more tender and carnal. Oyster shells could cut a gash in your throat big enough to eat the muscle. Big enough to slide the muscle down with no resistance. One of them moans about how good each bite is, growing more and more intense as the meal goes on. The other chuckles and moans as well. Pretty soon they can't be stopped. Both moaning and laughing hysterically over their food. It's cute. It's sexy. We are together again here at Monterrey's.

- Disco Tartare // Taste the raw passion of Murder City with a premium steak chopped to the rhythm of a four-on-the-floor. With beef raised ethically on our downtown rooftop pastures, and sauces minced and squeezed with the tenderness of a slow dance, you'll feel this one on your tongue for years to come.
- Fugu Paralysis // Experience the stun of sleep paralysis, fully conscious, with just a forkful from your dinner plate. Illegal in most cities, domestic and international, this delicacy is prepared with the utmost care so you can revel in a little danger.
- Oyster Death // Shells that could kill. Sea meat that can do the same.
- Demon's Caviar // As succulent as it is bitter, spice that bursts in your mouth. They'll know by your smile—that you're in Murder City!

HALLOWEEN: IT'S TIME FOR YOU TO OPERATE NOW

Everyone looked beautiful. It had all been fun and games up until that point, and now Halloween was just one big human body. But, the costumes were all the same as when I was younger. Witches, mummies, werewolves. But not me, I couldn't do that again. I was a teenage detective. But a dead one. Bullet hole in my eyeball and everything. And everyone at the Disco loved it–a lot of "Getta load of that kid with the eyeball!" Some even started to grind their teeth at me or walk on rotten legs in my direction.

But there was one costume that stood out against all the rest. Not because it was good but only because it was different, lame. One of the local drug dealers had dressed up like a doctor, too easy if you ask me. The costume itself was only a white coat over his shirtless torso. And he specialized in pain killers, so the cleverness was so spot on, and contrived, and I remember thinking it was a missed opportunity, that he could have been an undead doctor or whatever the fuck. But he never would have gone for that. I had always hated buying from him. Constantly standing at awkward angles, with his hips stuck out just right so you could tell there was a gun tucked into his pants underneath his shirt. But not tonight. No shirt meant there was only the gun, a snakeskin belt, and his abs. But, he was dancing like a motherfucker. I'll give him that.

I entangled myself into several clusters of dancers—this is before I knew how to dance–grapevining my way over to the doctor. But when he made eye contact with me, he pointed a sloppy finger in my face, told me that the doctor was off-call tonight. I'd have to get my pills from another practice across town. Then, he just sort of poked my forehead. I can still feel the flump of it against my skull. Dear god. He kept dancing.

I started shouldering my way toward the bar and found a circle of warlocks doing cocaine lines from a plastic knife. I did a bump and never saw them again. And a little bit of wandering later, I bumped into the bar where I saw Frankenstein waiting for a drink, twirling one of those–probably stolen–cocktail spoons between her fingers. Once we started talking, I noticed her stomach was painted green; the way she shook her squared shoulders was disconcerting every time, and even a little endearing. Star signs led to tarot banter and she mentioned something to me about how she draws the same card every time, her fate she keeps choosing, sleight of hand, pulling a card from the bottom of the deck. But the second she got down to the last drop of her drink, the doctor tapped on her shoulder. The fucker had been waiting. Said he'd have something else for her if she followed him to one of the back rooms. I hated him for his looks and I hated him for his lack of conversation. Could say so little and send a beautiful monster across the Disco. It was unnatural. My forehead gets all sweaty just thinking about it. Watching him take my friend away after we just met. See, I hadn't seen my neighbor and best friend, Steph, in months–not counting watching her get off the bus and go into her trailer–so that made Frankenstein my only friend at the time. I was so worked up, cocaine angry, that I almost missed it when she whispered to me, "Watch this, Netti," as she walked off into the crowd.

By the time I decided to go and knock on the door, and use my cocaine bravery to demand some pills, you could hear the laughing in the room, even over the music. It was like the hysterics were keeping time for the drum pattern that had been spinning itself away from the DJ. The door opened. At the back of the room were men in scrubs, muscles like the doctor. The man himself was to the side with Frankenstein. She looked over her shoulder at me, one of those looks that a guardian sibling might shoot you at a fucked up family reunion. A pharaoh and a mummy laid passed out in the corner. A pirate captain stacking all their empty drink glasses up to her chin.

I walked in, and no one really seemed to notice, not even the fish who opened the door. The doctor slouched against his chair, sliding down slowly until his stomach and torso were parallel with the ceiling. Flexed, he took Frankenstein's hand and invited her to feel his abs. Laughing as he grabbed a handful of pills from his coat pocket and sprinkled them over his stomach.

He takes the gun out of his pants, hands it to her. Says, "Hammer em' up! Do a line!"

She'd played him along so far, or she'd played that she'd played along, still playing if you think about it–you'll see. One more quick look at me to make sure I was watching, and then she started to let him have it. Like a sister berating her younger brother. Destroyed him. I would have been pretty demoralized myself. I've developed a pretty thick skin over the years, and I had one even back then, but I was pretty shocked by what she said. So abrasive it was almost cartoonish, rehearsed down to the most guttural of syllables. The doctor was just laying on the couch with illegal pills scattered across his abs. I knew what I had to do though.

Before he could sit up or collect his pills, I hit him with an 'I'll do it' and took the gun out of his hand. There was a tired cheer that came out of the others, like I was baby King Arthur stepping up to pull on Excalibur but they'd seen it a thousand times before. The gun was cheap too, flimsy, rickety, shiny as his ab muscles. The only reason it weighed anything at all was because it was packed with very real bullets.

Planted myself right between his legs, holding the pistol by the barrel. Now, I know nothing about guns. And up until that moment I'd had zero experience. But, I should have known–and probably did know, on some level–that this man was not the type to bother with a safety, that he'd get a big rush from never having it on, and always being dangerous. He was laughing, like a bully who didn't know what to say next. One of those looks like getta-load-of-this-kid. He was immortal.

The rubber eyeball glued on my face shook, even in that moment as I was motionless.

When the butt of the pistol hit his stomach, I could see his muscles go loose, like all the parts of the gun rattling around as I swung it. The hit left a red spot on his skin and I knew it would be purple in an hour. He wheezed, still laughing, gathering all the pills from the cracks of the cushions, piling them back onto his abs. He flexed again, the red spot screaming at me to hit him again. He was too. Do it, do it, do it, just fucking do it! The whole room, the men in scrubs, the pharaoh and mummy, the fish. They all chanted to just fucking do it. Crush the pills. Do a line.

I brought the gun down, hesitant this time. The pills bounced up just high enough to see the empty space between the doctor and the air of the back room. They landed, everyone sighing with disappointment. So I did it again, lazy again. Over and over. The gun parts clattering all around. More laughing, squealing even. I kept hitting him in the stomach, found a perfect rhythm. The clattering sound growing more pronounced and spaced out. Then it went bang.

The room was silent, except for the wet sound on the hard floor. After all these years the best way I could describe it is, you know when you vomit and it hits the water in the toilet bowl? Like that.

Then it was all screaming, and cutting coke lines to hold under his nose, but he was screaming too.

Naturally, I sobered up pretty quick—while they all circulated the room panicking, looking for things to help, water, towels, but all they found was more cocaine. I watched him do at least three lines after the gun went off. There was plenty going on, but what surprised me was that no one was mad. I just sort of circulated the room around with everyone else, looking under cushions too. Cocaine shock.

The blood had turned the chair black and brown and we were all frantic, like we'd seen an unexpected eclipse or something and were just trying to figure out if the world was going to end. Until he sat up. Stone-eyed and straight-mouthed. There was no more pain in the room, and our anxiety started to die down as his calm drifted through the air. He asked Frankenstein to please come stand beside him.

She had thread glued to her neck, to look like hack-job stitches. He was staring at the makeup, and then into her eyes. But neither of them saw the pupils of the other, just eyes dilated into some other blank space, like a vibrating, undulating place, where they're not strangers or dripping blood onto the floor.

So, he told her, "I need your thread."

"Fuck you."

"I have bled onto the floor. It needs to stop. You need to tie it off."

"My stitches aren't going to cut it."

"Please–"

"No," something about her tone shifts, like she's only looking at the doctor but speaking to someone else. "Because, honestly I believe you always knew this would happen. It's time to let it run its course. I know it hurts. I know it's not what you wanted. But this is it. This is how it takes place."

"But I always thought I could fight it, when the time comes...."

"But we know that's not the way this city works."

"What about him?" he asked with a bloody hole where his dick used to be. Something in the air broke and two of them were now clearly speaking to each other.

"He's the way things are, the violence that we've been hurtling toward this whole time."

"I don't under–" And something comes across his face, a thin layer of recognition, that he's had a version, or a version of a version, of this conversation before.

"He's a part of this just like we are."

"I'm not dying, am I?"

"No, you're about to operate, doctor," she presses the pistol between his eyes until there's a red imprint in his skin, takes a step back with the weapon still raised. "Serve yourself. Operate."

"We've gone so much further than this."

"It was never like this. You were never like this. It's time for you to operate now," she pulls the stitches from her neck. Skin glue hanging from the thread.

She had us. None of us could look away as she wrapped the thread between his fingers. His hands were steady too, no way they should have been, but that was her effect. She leaned over and whispered instructions in his ear. We only heard the bass outside the room, but the nodding of his head showed it was something familiar, something warm that he needed to be reminded of. She stood up and he took some deep breaths as he slid off his snakeskin belt. Frankenstein kicked the damn thing so it slid across the floor to me. I picked it up, not knowing why.

Then, needleless, he began the work of tying himself back together. Twisting. Wrapping. Looping. Knotting. We watched it all. Felt the temperature rise in the room. Listened for that minor little squelch noise, just to know that we were seeing something real.

He was tying off his final loop when Frankenstein leaned down close to me, "You're a good fucking detective, Netti" she says while she taps my bloody eyebrow, fake blood and real blood, with her fingernail. "A really good detective," she says.

Then she was gone.

I was leaving too. Without her, it was like the night had started over again. Everyone on the dance floor throwing up their arms in wild motions and howling like their throats were torn open, grinding up against each other, pivoting on their heels like only undead people do.

MAMBO ON THE RADIO

It's a stakeout, the kind Netti's seen on thin rolls of film. Detective Castra uses a pen knife to carve a small notch into the steering wheel, joining countless other marks that've made a rough road of the circle hung above her knees. Netti thinks about what these would mean if a different person made the cut, what kind of spells they could conjure instead of marked time.

Netti watches the sidewalk, so intently that he feels he can know what's around the corner of the block, up to three or four feet by vague impressions, shadows shaped criminally, quivering in and out of existence—they must be wearing wide hats and long coats. The radio between them crackles out a keyboard solo extending far beyond anything that's normally heard on popular stations, so much longer that it's beginning to invoke a fucked sense of the miraculous.

There's a dogwalker. Long fingers around the loop of the dog leash. It's leather. And there always seems to be some kind of slack even when the dog is pulling. It latches onto the collar with a small gold clasp and the dog seems to know the significance of the material. The dog walker is as tall as you would suspect with a proportionate coat. He's been making the rounds, circling this block for the length of their stakeout taking deep breaths of the city like it's good for his health.

Netti turns to Castra, "Did I tell you about the ad?"

She shakes her head, but that's the only indication that she's listening.

"They are going to play an ad for our show," he points to the radio buried in the monolithic dashboard. "It's basically an artist highlight. The agency folks I've been hanging around, they're airing a story about me and my work. And not just my art, but my story as a detective too. But it's mostly about the wolf and how I try to put myself into him, like I whispered for him to move and he did and now he's out on the city doing his own thing, solving his own crimes."

She smiles with half her mouth, "Do you think anybody will hear it? Radio's full of ghosts these days. Last I heard, all the kids want the real thing, the records, the DJ. That's why they're flocking to the Disco to get their throats cut."

Netti taps his fingers and knuckles on the dashboard to the rhythm of a mambo song, "Fuck you. I never minded ghosts." He thinks of the ad haunting through the city. Drifting through walls. An appearing and disappearing apparition to mark a key moment in the viewer's life.

There's a couple of bodies leaving a side door of the Disco. Netti can tell it's a drug deal before Castra. He likes this game, guessing what's between their palms. Starts with the eyes. The amount of white visible is an effective indicator. Between the two there's a casual amount of white, which gives him only a little, enough to steer him down the direction of an upper. So he waits a minute, and then two, for how many times they scratch behind their ears. Happens when people perform something in secret, he's found. But there are different categories of scratching—eager, concealing, to fill an awkward silence. This was none of the three usual categories—this one more like an attempt to draw blood. Uppers were right, uppers coming off of downers. These two knew each other well. This theory's confirmed when one reaches toward the other's face to remove a bit of food. These are good drugs that're being sold, something new. Nothing from before the demons. So, it's either flesh or feathers. He only needs to see the end of the interaction before he can tell which one.

One of them's singing lyrics to an old song, the other nodding along, both deeply trying to place the title. The lyrics start to run out, longer gaps between each one until eventually the last one falls from the singer's mouth. They both laugh politely and shrug a little, making peace with the fact that they may never be able to name that tune, and they disappear into the club. These people are flesh-eaters.

He's starting to wonder if, in another life, he's a vicious drug hound. And he wonders if Castra feels the same about herself. He wonders if he's not wondering at all, and he's known this all along, that the Killer isn't the point. But, he won't say a thing. Keep the performance going. He's the magician, baby. Drawing wolves for ghosts for a living.

Netti turns up the radio and turns toward the driver seat to see where Castra has her attention. She's staring at the gutter. There's still mambo on the radio but it's in its final chords. He reaches for the volume knob and turns it clockwise. The radio voice is quiet, stylized, maternal—the mom across the street inviting you and your disgusting friends to use her pool while she reads a murder mystery and empties a margarita. She lets the listeners know that they're in for another one—this one's by a band right here in Murder City. And a bass begins to play an absolute wormhole of a hyper-aggressive groove.

"Fuck. They're never gonna play it."

"Where do you think our killer might enter?"

"Has to be where that drug deal just happened."

"Netti, we're in a stakeout. You have to tell—where are you talking about?"

"It was self-evident. Right there at that door. You were staring at the sidewalk across the street or something."

"You saw where I was looking and didn't say anything?"

"It was self-evident. Plus, I would have told you if the Killer was coming through."

"Killers are obvious. I need you to point out the drug deals."

"I need you to acknowledge how long these songs are getting. All these fucking hours of bass and brass and sexy little choruses, but no ads. We've been here for hours and still haven't heard it. I need you to acknowledge that. That we're living in an age of no-commercials decadence and that's hard for the artists trying to get their work recognized for fucking once!"

"Netti, you're a great inbetweener. But you're here to help me find the Disco Killer. You know the club as good as anyone in there, but yours is the only head that's not half-packed full of cheap coke. Now, will you tell me next time you see a drug deal?"

He turns the volume back down, "The ad is gonna be big! I'm gonna get myself out there." He taps frantically against his temple, repeating himself, "Gonna. Get. Myself. Out there."

He stares out the windshield but not at the street.

"And you've made that point pretty clear now, asshole. I just need you to tell me what you're seeing when you're watching a criminal offense take place. Don't need to tell you again that the Killer is linked to the Murder City drug racket."

The post-chorus repeats for the third time. It has to be getting close. The dog walker materializes again and Netti points to the dog on the leash, "Am I supposed to also tell you if I see a loving thing walking on four legs instead of two. Would that be scandalously miraculous enough for you?"

"You know they've transported Feathers across the city in the stomachs of dogs, right? Something about their intestinal lining," she sighs. "It has no effect on them. They coat them in bacon grease and smear them across the floor. The dogs just lap it all up."

"I'm so fucking glad I could be a participant in your stakeout. It's just that I'm not sure I agree," he rolls down the window and thinks of smoking, what it'd be like to actually be able to blow smoke rings—what it'd be like if one of those smoke rings could float over and choke Castra around the neck. He lets his sentence trail off into nothing.

"There's a rat. Big one," Castra smiles, tracking the movement of a shadow in the gutter.

"I'm going to get a sandwich—anything for you?"

Eyes still on the rat, "Something marbled."

He pauses a second, "Does that mean bread or steak?"

"I won't know until you bring me one. And I'm not trying to be an ass. It's the only way."

The car door shuts on time with the beat of the radio.

Walking to the sandwich shop, he sees the spot where he stood as that couple died. Broken necks on the other side of the window. There's a stain where all the feathers fell on the floor. Someone's sitting right over it, tearing into a French Dipped as their platforms swing back and forth over the dark spot. Sauce drips down their fingers, drips onto the floor. Netti opens the shop door and the little bell rings.

He holds a paper bag over the center console between the two seats, "A Rueben."

"One of the better cuts this city has to offer," she takes the sandwich, unwraps it over the steering wheel. "Did you see anything? And I swear to Mother Mary's Mom's fucking syphilis if you say–"

"I didn't see any clues," his eyes scan for the right words. "No evidence."

The sound of the Disco swells. On the sidewalk, where only the bass had reached, the guitar chords and thumped lyrics begin to sharpen in the air and make their shape obvious. Netti knows this one. It's a great song. Sexy.

The two men, the dealer and the buyer, emerge out of the alley, having remembered the song. And now they're singing it together with their eyes rolled back. Singing against the other song happening now. Stretching an unapologetic slow jam over a suave barn burner. Castra, she sets the Reuben on the dashboard—and Netti can only imagine she's seen the whites of their eyes. With the slam of the door, she's striding toward the two with her hand on her nightstick. Seeing nothing but the punishment ahead, tangling herself in the dogleash, unaware that she'd set the dog free from its golden collar. By the time the man in the coat has called out for his Snapper for the second time, she's dropping her nightstick on the dealer's collarbone with a dog leash wrapped around her ankle.

But, the sound's still coming out of the side door. The lyrics are clapping along faster now, vanishing the moment they expose themselves to the street.

"Snapper, drop that! Snapper!"

Netti feels something. It's heavy, like his guts are a scale and something massive's been dropped down on them, slamming instantly to the bottom—his teeth, after numb calculations, register the answer.

It's a mask.

The Killer's splattered, lightly, surprisingly, with blood lopes into the alley. The blade still humming in his hand.

"When life gives you lemons, make lemonade. When life gives you pickles, well, make a murder mystery. That's what our zaniest wolf detective always has to say.

"Oh my FUCKING God!" Netti screws the volume knob to the max as he leaps out of the car toward the alley.

Castra's choking the drug buyer with the leather dog leash, calling him a horrible thing, the dealer unconscious and broken at her feet. Saliva strings from his mouth, distorting the asphyxiated purple of his skin.

The song's still picking up, reaching a speedy plateau—no dancing to be heard inside. The Killer's cleaning his blade on his suit, making a move of the motion. Netti hates it, but there's a real sex appeal to his dancing. Bloodying his suit. The blade never getting clean. Tonight's mask is made of something white, dark, splintered, marbled. Not his favorite, but one he'd certainly chase if this mask was on a demon instead of a killer.

"JOIN US SATURDAY MORNING TO SOLVE THIS MUR-DER WITH OUR ZANIEST DETECTIVE."

Netti turns back to the car, story-less. The dog's slinging a dead rat between his teeth and the man in the coat can't get him to stop.

STEPH DECAPITATES

Steph strikes the man's jaw with a stiletto. The dancers on the floor around them cheer at the sight of blood and flesh wounds. The man, balding by the second, holds a bony hand against the bleeding, stumbles his way off the floor as dozens of open palms slap his ass in a club form of poetic justice. A kid with a mohawk the length of his spine runs to Steph and speaks what must be a congratulations in her ear, then raises his hand like a prizefighter who's just become champ. Blood drops from the raised stiletto onto both their foreheads. The braids of her hair drum at her shoulders as the crowd closes in around her, shaking her frame in the tone of Congratulations, you've got her!

The store is blurred with pink, purple, and green nebulas of false neon lights, clambering off of plastic keepsakes. For the first time in this demon wave, Steph takes note of the tourist souvenirs exploding out of the shelves. Mugs with the faces of Feathers, and Pretty Faces, a word bubble with Whisper Teeth typography spelling out obscenities that only appear when the mug is hot. There are portrayals of demons in the style of saints from orthodox iconography, emaciated, looking toward heaven, wounded by their own way of believing. There are t-shirts with oversized lettering that read "I SURVIVED MURDER CITY" and "DIE ON THE DANCEFLOOR!" Poorly designed book covers penned by local authors documenting the lore of their neighborhoods and boroughs. There's another bookshelf and it's filled with only one title, *The Discotheque through the Decades: A Study of Murder City Disaster Cycles*. She remembers this one from school, but nothing inside it—only the teacher who assigned it.

She left it in her locker every night it was assigned. But her teacher wouldn't even touch the text either, only going into tangents vaguely related to the content between its covers. Only moments after the bell rang, he once told them a story about him and his brother and their ongoing feud with their nextdoor neighbor. Of course, they were young and they certainly committed minor terrors against the man and his property. One could make an argument for his animosity, his teacher's logic would continue. After work each day, he'd busy himself with the labors of his kitchen. He and his brother had noticed through the window, entranced with the process of fat washing. There, he'd fire up his stove with exorbitant amounts of bacon, only to toss them to the side and pour the smoking grease into a bowl full of bourbon. Swirling a wooden spoon around in the mixture, he then let it sit for an hour or two. He'd carry the bowl to the ice box out back and leave it for a full day. The neighbor kids hated this. When the waiting was done, he'd carry the bowl between his arms back to the kitchen at the front of his home. Meticulously, he'd scrape the fat that had congealed at the top of the drink. Then he would strain the mixture through coffee filters with an effort that felt pastoral and almost romantic. He then took the bowl of bourbon back to the icebox to chill a little further. When he came back to the kitchen, he dumped the bacon grease into a cardboard box, walked it to his front curb and dropped it beside his trash can for the city to pick up in the morning.

But they would get there before the city. Waiting for him to go back to the icebox to try his latest creation, Steph's future teacher and his brother sprinted to the box of grease, whispering, swearing until they made it safely to their house. It wasn't long until he drank half of the bottle and the drink sent him to sleep in the living room. And they returned with the box.

With open hands full of grease, they smeared demonic symbols and lyrics of popular rock 'n' roll songs across the hood, windows, and doors of his car. In the middle of the words, the grease would thin into nothingness and the next letters would be thick with globs of it. By morning, the grease had caught innumerable ants and dark birds plucked at their resigned thoraxes.

Steph's future teacher and the brother missed the school bus that morning, hiding in the bushes to watch his reaction. He'd run onto the lawn, barefoot, shotgun pointed at the sky. The blast went off the second the school bus drove by. The birds were gone by the time the police arrived, but the ants were nibbling at the feathers they left behind in the grease.

So he filled his shotgun full of rocksalt. And he filled the air with its spray of minerals the next day. It stung deep in their skin. They still feel it when laughing their way through the story years later.

But the story moves around school about an old newspaper clipping that some student found—that it wasn't rock salt in the shotgun and the brother actually got a hole punched through his chest. Shreds of lung and heart opened up to the insects. That he had to chase the birds away from his brother's body until a silent ambulance arrived.

In the back of the store, Steph reaches the wall of blades. Each one reflects iridescent light from the glow that lies in front of them, from the demonic displays and storefront signs. She would try them all out, weigh them in her hand, swing them through the air, maybe test out a stabbing motion. But there is only one that she actually wants. In another story, it would call out to her. Something about it reminded her of a movie she used to watch with Netti.

Her knuckles don't even turn white when she squeezes the hilt under her fingers. There are feathers etched into the blade and a sloppily cast demon on the pommel. It's cheap, but clearly sharp as shit and she could tell the second she walked into the store. Lethal. But light enough to keep in bed at night.

The receipt is as long as the sword and she folds it carefully, tucks it into the pocket of her jeans. The coffee shop across the street is out of coffee. She leaves without getting anything at all, the sword strapped medievally to her back. She was going to sit on the curb, thinking about the way the coffee burned its way down her throat and she would have traced the outgoing warmth all the way to her fingertips. This is practice.

Instead, she finds herself standing on a trashcan at the top floor of a parking garage. Six stories up, she can brace her body against the minor shocks of windchill. She focuses on her skin and how it recoils against the slight cold, how well it clings to her bones in all situations. Then the wind gets underneath. Pretty soon it's a part of the muscle and reaching into the bone. She observes the sensation drifting through her bloodstream. It splashes into her brain.

She visits with a memory. The corner of her best friend's smile. The disco ball spouting red reflections down on the crowd when they were at the edge of being kids, the only time she went to the disco. Sweat and quaaludes in the air. Unsure, she returns to the feeling in her fingertips. The breeze has switched directions. Then stillness.

Another memory. The alley's wet on the asphalt and in the air, loud with boys wearing purple and teal-stained shirts handing over joints to Netti outside the bagel shop. It's only a minute before they're both lighting up and the dealers are gone. Her eyes burn and Netti isn't anywhere that she can see. There's something about the taste that reminds her of her first job, the feeling she'd get when she'd have to tell a customer, "No, sorry. We don't have that here." The slippery mass of regret she'd somehow carry with those words.

Back to the parking lot and she's no longer cold. Steph's chest hurts. She thinks about why and starts to leave.

She lays in bed, her sword across her chest with both hands on the hilt. With slow, meditated breaths, she feels the blade rise and fall. For the last forty-eight hours, she hasn't let herself sleep so he can fall full force into a state of unconsciousness. Her entry should be quick enough to bring the attention of a demon.

For a moment, she falls too deep. Her stomach rises to her throat. Her feet are somewhere in the middle of her shin bones. There is nothing tangible that she can see. Only some kind of movement surrounding her, or innumerable instances of kinetic energy. It makes a terrible rustling. With a deep breath, she observes the sensation of her stomach sinking back to its rightful place as she rises out of her point of entry.

There's a demon on either side of her bed.

She's paralyzed, but she can feel the hilt's leather and the friction of its roughness against her palm and fingers. She's focused on the feeling in her hands as the demons turn toward each other, as if they just noticed that the other had also arrived. Quickly, they stand up on the foot of the bed—more energy than Steph had imagined they would show. There's a rehearsal to their motions. They've done this somewhere else. One lifts up both hands like a lighter in the wind. The other leans its face toward the imaginary flame, expands its chest as if to inhale, its fingers crowded around where its mouth would be, clutching a thin roll of imaginary tobacco.

The leather is rough under her hands. The hilt of her sword is steady. Only the faintness of her breathing moves the blade.

The demon with the cigarette takes long drags. It drops its hands to its waist and tilts its head toward the ceiling to mimic the exhaling of smoke. Then long drags. Minute-long drags. The next one is over eager to perform. It cups its mouth with the other's hands nested closely. It tries to expand its chest as if to inhale, but instead enlarges its back with balloon-like roundness.

She knows she can't move. Can just feel the hilt of the sword.

Their routine continues—lighting invisible crack pipes, holding spoons over needles and injecting heroin into each other's tied-off arms. They do it all with the sloppily mimed movements of children. Steph begins to feel a loosening in her arms, the loosening felt in the insides after vomiting. The demons have collapsed on the bed in a playful imitation of blacking out.

Next, she's able to draw her feet up to her waist, and then sit up at the head of the bed. Her sword lays across her knees. Her spine rests at a natural curve. She thinks about breathing. The demons quiver with convulsing giggles, trying to stifle their laughter for the sake of their game. It's evident they're full of joy, that they don't see each other often.

She stands over them, the blade at her side, its point hovering around her ankle bone.

The first one, Steph decapitates. Guts-colored vertebrae spill from the void of its neck. They flood the bed and pour over the edges, clatter angrily against the wooden floor. Suddenly aware of Steph, the other leaps back but her blade lands squarely where its face would be. It cups its hands around the sword. And shakes with a brief laugh.

Steph, with movement coursing through her arms, doesn't feel anything at all.

SHOWER DEATH!

He turns the shower knob all the way to the left, always lets it heat up for five minutes before entering. Enough time to brush his teeth with a newly opened toothbrush, and scrub the head of the faucet with the old-looking one. Steam starts to fog the mirror, rises thickly over the magenta curtain. He pulls it back.

A demon with no real eyes, only feathers packed into his sockets, stands in the falling water. Seems to enjoy the heat. Like standing in the soft orange of a younger sun. Water runs from the corner of its mouth, smooth on one side and reptile-like on the other. The shoulders seem to be made of thin lumps of cartilage, smooth, hardened under a heavy gravity. His feathers are drenched, starting to droop a little down his face.

The only thing he can feel is the toothbrush in his hand. His teeth. His spine. Skull. Knuckles. Ribs. Sternum. It's all evaporated into some kind of bristling defensive energy channeled into his right hand.

It didn't normally go this way.

The demon tries to tuck the feathers up back into his skull, still not noticing the intruder. Netti slips back behind the curtain, holding the brush to his chest. In the open space, water spritzes out onto the vinyl floor. A puddle starts to appear, soaking into the pink rug at his feet. The sounds of the waters start to shift, striking different areas of the shower. The Feather is moving, knocking over a bottle of shampoo. The boom of the impact disorients the deep insides of his ears.

The human intruder waits—until a dense, dripping head peeks out from around the corner of the curtain. With one breathless movement,

Netti plunges the toothbrush deep into its eye socket. It lets out a cry that sounds like glass cracking, falling back into the shower, taking the curtain down with it. Netti breaks out of the bathroom and bumbles down the hall, trying different doors to see where he could hide or grab a weapon.

He settles for a wood-paneled room of taxidermied birds. Pictures of the house's family smirk down at him, clawed feet pointed upward from their tight fists, beaks opened slightly at the forest floor.

He'd followed a Pretty Face out of the city, hoping for a mask. But he drifted with his following distance and lost track of the demon at the edges of his old neighborhood. When he realized where he was, he felt like his guts were in two separate locations at once and the dizziness made his eyes roll back. The whole trailer park had been flattened. He knew this. But he hadn't seen the development since they built perfect square homes on top of the grounds. With a pocketful of quaaludes he'd found on the sidewalk when making rounds at the Disco with Castra, he started with one and then two and fell asleep in the pine needles outside of the neighborhood.

Over the next few days, he watched the family inside the home where he might have once lived—it was difficult to tell. They were packing. Bags spilling from the mouth of their station wagon in the driveway. The bags were creased and scuffed, no luxury, just the signs of extensive travel. That they weren't tied to this city in a meaningful way.

When the family pulled out of their driveway, Netti brushed the pine needles from his coat and he approached the house.

Something's dragging in the hall. It's like wind outside, but synthetic.

The demon drops feathers from its eye as it drags the shower curtain across the carpet. Stops, kneels, to pick them up, put them back inside, careful to pack gently around the toothbrush still lodged snugly into the skull. It stands back up, loses more, stoops again. That's the process, repeated, patient.

Netti sees the string hanging from an attic trap door, counting the average time it spends gathering wet feathers back into its head. There's time. So he waits for the next kneel, slides back into the hallway and lowers the attic door to his extended arm. Pulls himself up, only creaking the hinges slightly, no louder than the weather outside. From the attic, he shuts the door softly, glimpses the Feather rising to its feet again through the crack.

The darkness is heavy like the glue they pour into the plywood that forms the flooring all around him. All except for four dim orange lines of light, an air vent letting in the glow of a nearby streetlight. He listens for the incremental dragging. But it stopped. In the attic, he wonders if the Feather found what he was looking for, or finally gathered all its feathers.

Everything is static, and nothing marks the time up there. Not until light floods, briefly, through the vent in the side paneling. Then the sound of car doors, the absence seeming to be something between a long weekend and full vacation.

The distant sound of the front door closing. A conversation between the family, garbled at first, growing in clarity. Numbers and words, like "Quail," begin to materialize through the barriers between them. He cracks the attic door, sees an empty hallway. There are so many doors where the Feather could disappear. He could warn them, an intruder surprising a hunting family with news that something else is in their house. Or he could wait, see what happens.

An unknowable amount of time. Then the first gunshot. Closer. Screaming. Up the stairs as far as the Netti can tell. Then in the hall. Right below him. He cracks the attic door again, the blasts growing louder.

Closes it. Waits.

Opens again, more this time. The feathers dragging the curtain down the hall. The gunshots land holes in it. Particles drift out his wounds, feathery things, moving like dust motes gliding upward at curved angles.

Closes again, feels around in the dark for an escape, long enough to find that the vent is steel and lodged into the frame of the house. No getting out except for the ladder.

The gunshots pick up the pace, desperate, the cadence of a drunken Vaudeville tap dance. By the sound of it, there's no aiming involved, just open fire. Peaks through the attic door. Only the wrapped-tight head of a man being strangled by a shower curtain, eyes bouncing around in their sockets until they're so swollen they can't swell any more. More feathery particles swell into the air as he straddles, unmoving, over his victim. Netti shuts it as quickly as he can do so quietly, not sure if any have drifted into his dark hiding space. Careful to breathe only as much as needed, fearing ingestion of the particles. But that can only last as long as it does.

A few more shots, and then it's silent. Just the intruder and the attic. The orange lines are incoming, just dawn light, no cars pulling into the drive away to see what the noise is all about. It's warm. The insulation feels surprisingly soft, speckled with the feather particles, compelling him to grab it by the handful and raise it to his face, breathing in the softness of it–good drugs. No reason behind his movements, logic or rules. Only interminable comfort like hot water. No visitors. No families. He can't be reached up here. Netti's safe, so safe that nothing outside of the attic could possibly touch him, even if he left the space entirely. It's like he's back under the shed on Halloween. The thought makes his scars feel warm on his face.

There was no way for him to know for how long he waits in the attic, but at some point the comfort hits a critical mass. Makes him feel like it's safe to leave. He lowers the door. Steps down the ladder, not quietly, only softly, comfortably.

He steps off the ladder and onto the bodies of the family. Careful not to trip over their limbs.

The Feather is at the other end of the hallway. Reaches to the toothbrush in its eye socket, wraps his fingers around it like something familiar by now.

Slowly, almost lazily, it pulls the brush out from its skull. A creaking squelch comes with the movement. But it's something else now. The feathers have hardened into a long, dark, grizzly, grotesquely sharpened point—as if they'd hardened under a heavy gravity.

Something about the sharp object reminds Netti that he came here for a mask. And if Feathers don't have masks, then maybe he could make one.

The visitor and the intruder each walk down the hall, with no way to know how long it takes to meet in the middle, for the toothbrush point to slice across Netti's face, tracing a healed scar in red, for Netti to imagine his face as a face full of teeth. To sink his human incisors in the face of the demon

It tastes like sweat and he opens his mouth for another bite, enough to grip the skin with his molars. And pull. He pulls until the face peels enough for him to see inside the head. Shapeless in there, a fluid, or substance moving without intention around the shape of the head. The only thing resembling any kind of structure is a small square. A cardboard box falling to pieces in the moisture. Each shred that's pulled away reveals more definite shapes and sharp angles. A little stack of razor blades, the smell of rubber, the presence of shame so heavy it feels like a friend.

It's time to leave the house.

ALL HE SEES IS PURPLE

They watch from the sidewalk as the men in blue coveralls paste the last of the sign to the billboard. The letters were nocturnally purple, wavy down the sides.

WHERE HELL IS HOME

It stands at the edge of the city, facing past its limits. Duplications would scatter across highways from there with directions on where to find the nexus of demonic activity. 50 Miles till Death. 27 Miles - Then It's Too Late. Only 1 Left…The chief creative officer of the last marketing agency in the city wipes the sweat of last night's disco from his upturned forehead, "I think this is going to work."

The two interns set up their desks in the apartment at the city's edge, perched above the expressway that barrels past the billboard. With un-zipped backpacks, they pile blank notepads onto the surface of their shared desk. It's too large for the studio office, only room enough to squeeze between the desk edge and the wall. There's a movie poster tacked above them, a man and a woman dancing in mauve and yellow, hung up only as a point of conversation between themselves and their creative officer who mentioned the movie more than once in their group interview process.

Their job is to tally the number of cars motivated by the billboard campaign. And their job is to be generous in their calculations. They were asked to do the same thing weeks ago, before the new purple letters were pasted to the billboard. It was the same time of day, preceding a weekend, enough time after work to have packed up the family and hit the road. Their numbers were hazy then. The two weren't able to decide on a system they felt confident in, as they switched between sheets to start over, but, looking back, they weren't sure of which numbers carried over from the sheet before and which numbers began with the new sheet. Tonight, the system's set. They're committed to using one sheet and one sheet only, tracking entrances from the city in the top right corner of the paper and exits on the bottom left. They weren't supposed to track exits. That's above and beyond. They're collecting data.

But, the issue is that they're bored. Bored until they begin to make out again, the first time since the first time they did this sort of thing. So, they make out with their eyes closed, a smoldering joint keeping an orange watch over the passing cars. Cars that would later be remembered as only the most rudimentary of estimates. By the time it's a full open-mouth make out, one of them opens their eyes. The cars are all the same color and they wonder if it's the weed. The other explains that weed doesn't do that sort of thing, that they've run upon a statistical anomaly. They kiss a little more passionately, like a borealis had hung itself above their head, but then all the cars pass and their lips part with a little string of saliva stuck between them.

And so they finish the joint, pass it between the other until it's three joints later and they haven't seen any cars enter the city. This is good for reporting. It seems that most of the inbound traffic is related to tourist hour travels. But, the anomaly, their shitty little miracle, isn't coming back. Not yet at least.

Their last joint is replaced by a spliff and pretty soon it's just cigarettes and just friends for the summer as they're really just here for the professional experience.

"It's actually been a great time to join the industry." The man has slicked back hair like plastic onyx. "Not many acupuncturists left after the demons came. And, with the more – well, there's no other way to say it – horse shit clinics gone, so are some of the policies that were never meant to be a part of the art form. It had really stagnated the process for so many students of the craft, and it was frankly hard to see. I know I'm pretty new to the art, but I was getting pretty fed up with what I was seeing. So much focus on litigation, and counter-litigation, and waivers, and blood oaths, and whatever the hell they write up next. It was all just make-believe court dates. No more needles. No more skin. Just malpractice suits that very well may never happen.

And, obviously, client safety is a huge priority for us. Because it's a priority of the art form. Because there's no danger in it. Not if you know what you're doing. If you've actually studied it the right way, and are willing to take the right risks.

Did you know some schools don't even let you push a needle in before you complete their program? You have to leave before you can stick it in. Fucking crazy if you ask me. You only learn by actually committing your body to the motion. There's no other way to go about it really. That's how real art is made anyway.

But yeah, you might be wondering about my process. I like to explain everything once I've got the needles in. That way you can learn about the benefits as you're actually experiencing them. It's one of the new developments that I'm particularly excited about. It's certainly not the old way of doing things.

So, what you'll start feeling is a little bit of warmth starting to gather itself around your eyes. That's one of the early signs of improved circulation, and it's going to make those puffy eyes flatten down into marble. The results are insane. I think you're going to be really happy if you stick with it for a few weeks. And not just the puffy part. All those dark lines are going to vanish as well. I've heard people say that it's like they look their age again. People our age who look way older from missing out on all that sleep. It's understandable. We're in Murder City.

But, you have to take the steps to take care of yourself. And, you have to take them consistently. Otherwise, what's the point? If there's no progress, you only have to look in the mirror to figure out why. It's tough. I get it. That's why I started studying acupuncture. That was my own progress. My own evolution. And look at me now. I honestly never would have thought that I'd be here. Not without increasing my circulation.

First, in here..." he points to his chest. And he points to his head. He continues.

But Vega's going cross-eyed. Seeing double past the needles stationed around her eyes. She would have loved to stop it. To interject, lead the conversation somewhere. But, she's paralyzed.

She fell out quicker than she would have expected. All of it adding to a quick doze off. But, she was awake just as quickly. Trying to decide if the demon outside the window is one or two. How many needles it's pulling from its face. The more needles it removes, the less features you see. More blankness across skin. More needles on the sidewalk.

She's made a real art of this. Summoning the interesting ones. Putting bodies through motions.

Netti thought they were going to the Disco. He follows the Mixing Boys into an apartment building several blocks away from the club. Some boys go up the stairs and others descend. He hangs around the ground floor, noting the color of their socks going up, the texture of their hats going down. It's humid in the building. The walls are damp and there's mold spreading from the air vents. The elevator stays in the lobby, unmoving, a belly full of rusted wires inside.

For a while the number in the basement outweighs the number on the floors upstairs. Like the building's gravity was pulling them all down slowly into its divet in space-time. Netti's been given a bag of feathers, told to make the delivery at a door two floors up. They sit so dry, scratching around in a match box. There's a cheap design on the face of the match box, a little blue disco ball, and when Netti shakes around the feathers it's like the ball is about to shatter into a handful of pieces.

He slides open the box. The feathers are a dehydrated brown with small streaks of blue and purple, flecks of yellow. He does junkie math. Estimating the quickness of the high by volume and weight. Making comparisons from his old drugs.

There seems to be a critical mass and all the Mixing Boys start to boil back out of the basement. He hears a "Netti, move your ass," and he's back in the middle of them all. Bouncing up the stairs with the others, manic upward movement, flight by flight until they're all standing around a green door with a gold knocker hung over its pinhole–a dark absence in a blank emerald of enclosure, exclosure, depending on what's on the other side of the door. A knock, a pause, two knocks, long pause–like the knocking is done–one more double-knock.

"You know where the door knob is!"

On the inside of the apartment, it's even more humid than the downstairs lobby. The brown and orange geometries of the wallpaper swell out past any negative spaces of yellow. Condensation gathers around the thin Halloween scars on Netti's face. They pass through a living room fortified with burn sunset-style cushions and woven light fixtures that seem to actively lower themselves into the eyes of the visitors. A vinyl-floored kitchen opens up to them, hazy with the source of the humidity. He feels nothing.

There's a woman, with the patience of a long-beaked crane, holding a thermometer in the boiling water, a thick joint between her lips, its smoke blending with the heat of the water in some sort of alchemical reaction, swirling, turning the air into a liquid itself, purple at first, growing more clear as the two amalgamate.

The Director speaks through tight lips, careful not to drop the long ash of the joint in the water, "Over the ocean, they're crazy about this method. Say it'll be in every kitchen in the west in the next five to ten years. I don't buy it. I'm crazy about it too–they're right about the science of it. But, it won't catch on."

"You don't have to explain the economical impact of the demon onslaught. We sell drugs, for Christ's sake!"

"No no, I see where your head is at, but I'm not talking about the economy. I'm talking about indulgence, the sacrilegious sizzling that turns us on every time a slab hits the grill," a purple breath exits from her nostrils and clarifies in the air around her.

"It's hard to beat indulgence," a Mixing Boy hands her a plastic bag full of crushed brown powder, "What are you making?"

"It's a cold, sexless method for making a perfectly bloody steak," she takes a drag and the veins of her eyes glow purple for the length of a few breaths.

"You had me at 'hot and sexy.'"

"The problem with you Mixing Boys, you never listen."

"What good would we be if we only carried on our professional arrangement in nothing but a transactional manner? Talk about cold."

She places the thermometer on the counter and lifts a steaming plastic bag out of the pot. A dark slab sealed at the bottom of it. Netti's sick to his stomach, but it's the sober kind.

Mercury reaches up to the 98° mark in the thermometer, begins to lower on the particle board counter.

She turns to the lead Mixing Boy, "You only brought Feathers?"

"You went through all of the meat already? We brought you a full carcass' worth last week!"

"For this to work, I need to burn through it in excessive amounts. Nauseating, back-breaking excess. This isn't the time for measuring by the millimeter, or weight by the gram. This is a matter of breaking down the fucking door."

The street lights thrum against the asphalt. Netti's scanning the windows for near-sleepers tucking themselves into bed. Two women in evening gowns kiss beside a piano the size of their studio apartment. An old man reads a tome by the light of his tobacco pipe. A sweatered pair of parents shovel toys under a bunk bed, a pair of identical twins in paisley pajamas switch between the top and bottom bunk in a blur. A woman in the posture of grieving sets the table for herself.

Netti has a feeling about the old man. Tamping down the burning leaves of his pipe, thumbing a translucent page streaked with dark lines of sacred geometry. One pull—and a puff of smoke the size of his face. He hangs the pipe nimbly on an ornamental stand on his bedside table. Picks up a bell jar an inch thick and places it gently over the pipe. The small ember inside it brightens briefly until it's nothing. He lays his head down on the pillow with a nightly, or ritualistic, or sacramental, heavy cough. His bedroom door opens as he stares at the ceiling, not moving, still awake.

The demon walks in with familiarity. No show in its movements, or anything like confidence, only footsteps it traces each night, like a musician might lay her fingers on all the right places of her first flute. And then it waits, with its back turned at the foot of the bed. The man stares at the ceiling, adjusting himself in the bed at the added weight of the visitor. He alternates between his back and his side a few times before falling asleep with his back to the window.

It's another good mask. Simple, but original. Large splinters stitched down in harsh horizontal lines. The gauzy fabric has been shredded at various points all around the head, giving it an organic sense of facial features in places where no one possesses them.

He counts the numbers of windows leading vertically up to the apartment, then counts across the building to pinpoint the door he'd have to wait outside of. On his way through the apartment, he passes by as she lowers a steamed slice of meat in the incision of a Mixing Boy's leg, his screams terrible, blurring in on themselves, liquid echoes as she uses a pair of tongs to push the meat down deeper. Netti wonders what new flesh might feel like underneath his own, if he'd be able to stop after just one slice.

He feels nothing at all. For the rest of the night, he won't feel anything at all.

When Netti enters the room, he thinks of his Steph's cat—how it would walk on his chest at night, picking up its paws and pressing them back down again and again. That's what the demon was doing with small, dull feet. Stepping in place, one foot at a time, on the sleeper's chest. The man's torso was thin and exhaled with a narrow circumference, but the demon stayed balanced as it turned in slow circles in the place that it had chosen. It was like imbalance wasn't a concept to its body, like it couldn't sense shakiness or trembling on any physical or emotional level. The sleeper moaning weakly in his sleep, weak enough to build unexpected resentment inside of Netti. It was something fragile, something that could be cut down.

At the edge of the bed, picking at the sheets, estimating the thread count, he wonders how these visits affect people to the extent that they do. He once heard a story of a man who got so sick of his demon, that he started visiting the demons of his neighbors. He'd provoke them in his neighbors' rooms and lure them out to the hallway. There, he did the only thing he knew to do and he tried to light them on fire. They burned but didn't burn up, nothing about their form changing in the flames. He screamed, out of fear, but mostly out of helplessness. Stressed the demons out so much that they pinned him down and shoved one of their flaming slender hands into his throat. His neighbors described the event as having the distinct smell of burning gums.

This room smells like pipe smoke. Something cut down far off and dried for burning in a place far from this city. The demon steps on the man's chest, at slower intervals now. Making concerted effort to squeeze out more air with the natural rising and falling of the man's breathing. Netti's time will come soon. He finds the movements of the mask to be even more fluid than he could see from across the street. It rattles softly, with the charm of a simple percussion instrument. The time's getting pretty close. The sleepy man wheezes, a thin sheet of wet sounds splitting from the back of his throat. It's a wonder his ribs aren't cracking. Netti heard the dull pops of dozens of rib cages. The air's metallic with the weight of exhaling with no inhale. It's time.

The Pretty Face turns to Netti. They always do. And, not caring, it arches its back, falls back until it catches itself on the headboard. Its body stretched tightly into a half crescent, dangling its head like something that's gotten loose from the influence of gravity's stabilizing forces. Netti's best guess is that this is how they breathe it all in. The paralysis itself. Catching it all with its sail of a spine. The rattling head is euphoric. Jostling in every direction. Striking the sleeper on the chin, drawing a thin patch of crimson across the points of contact.

Netti's window arrives. He tightens his snakeskin belt a notch and steps up on the bed, places a foot on either side of the man, and stands over the oblivious demon. This is the part he dislikes. The leathery chalk texture of the demon's legs. The blade-like hip bones jutting out from under the skin. The awful spiral pattern of its abdomen, spiraling in both directions, stretched as tight as a horizon across its body. The ribs that seem to be anchored to nothing, narrow fingerling islands drifting through the torso. Its arms as thin as its neck stretching to the headboard. He climbs it all. Slowly, but trusting of the demon's strength. He kneels on its chest, as it stands on the chest of the man.

The mask has to be taken from the top. He's tried from below, but that puts needles in your ear canal; something comes out of you when the demon bends over and you go under. The best method is to climb on top while the demon is in its succubus state and reach under its torso. The dangling of the head is always difficult, no patterns, only euphoric movements, unmeasurable, dark geometries. He lowers his hands.

The head's violent. Whatever it's getting from this experience, it's lurid, fracturing. It's something that'll make you want to tear something else, a way to make the feeling or energy some kind of tangible—even if it means tearing yourself. Netti lets his finger tap against the head whenever it moves in their direction, getting a read of the quickness of its neck and the harshness of its angled movements.

He's also getting a feel for the mask, where it ends and how it's fastened. On lucky days and nights, he'd hook his index or stake his thumb through a loop or a buckle and feel the mask come undone in the movement. But, he's come to find that the only time to expect this is when their arms are actually thinner than its neck, presumably from growing strong in the sublunary atmosphere. Most demons are young. Most have no way to take off their mask.

He's safe on top, but he enjoys the feeling of dropping his hands into the demonic effects below. It puts a pang of excitement underneath his fingernails. He feels them sliding, just slightly, under the mask. There's rippling under the skin of its neck. This isn't good. Rippling means an emotive demon, normally only ever flashing across its face. A rippling throat means consequences for afterward. It's like tendons snapping shut directly underneath the layer of skin. From the best Netti has deduced, this is a purely aesthetic function, that they don't seem to communicate with one another at all, only across themselves. He lowers his finger further underneath the mask and the rippling becomes more rubber, fluid, and simultaneously inorganic, mechanical, moving outward in hard-angled shapes. It's so dry–fingernails cracking through flakes of cracking skin. Further, until his wrists are entering under the mask. That's where it stops, no room for him to go further. Though the demon's still oblivious because of whatever he's draining from the man on the bed.

It's awful every time, what he has to do at this part of the steal. He stretches his arms as far as they'll go, pressing the side of his face against the demon's chest. There's nothing like human organs on the inside. Humans have squelching and pumping, the pumping and exchanging of fluids. In the demons, there's a dry rattling. Like dead seeds scattering through a dried gourd. Shrivelled leaves slapping at the sidewalk. The writhing of the demon's head is starting to catch what may be its version of a pattern, nothing predictable but something Netti can trace, to feel on a deep level. Its skin starts to feel softer in its hands, almost like they're communicating across planes. He draws his palms together just slightly, just enough to clamp a hold of its head and slow its movement. Just a little more pressure and he can make it stop. He presses with his fingers too. Shaking his knuckles, pushing his fingertips deep into its unbreaking skin. Then there's no movement. This is the part he enjoys.

His hands snap into an uncontrollable motion. Whatever series of movements the demon just performed, his hands repeat in a ghostly cho-reography. His fingers brush against skin, gathers the mask together in knots. Stretching out at the free patches of air. All until it's off the demon. Hanging loose in his hands, as unliving and glorious as if he'd torn out a breathing organ. The demon presses its faceless expression into the man's. Rippling its skin around. At this point the demon always takes out the pain of the loss of influence on the victim himself. He thrashes and flails against the man, who's now far from paralyzed. He's flailing too. The skin of the Pretty Face ripples against the man, filling in all the contours of his human face structure. The demon's skin growing looser and looser until it's lapping at the man's flesh with enough force to break the skin. Small gaps at first. Lapping, lapping, lapping. The gaps grow wider, then longer. The skin's coming off entirely as Netti forces himself to look away this time.

He leaves the building with the new mask folded carefully in his coat pocket. Across the street, the Mixing Boy with an incision verticalled up his thigh is dancing with all the conviction of a man born for the disco dancefloor. Unreal amounts of body weight on his wounded leg, blood somehow only dribbling, spritzing out into the air. The woman from the kitchen sits on a stoop, clapping, keeping time with nothing but the visage of a proud, proud mother. The other Mixing Boys are pulling spare change from their pockets at a pretzel cart lurching over the gutter of the street. The screams, of the victim and the demon, are louder in Netti's head than usual. But, this is something else he loves about masks. He loves that Pretty Faces have no eyes–their masks have no holes.

Moments later, he's slumping in an alley, contorting his body to fit into a hiding space behind loose bricks and a heating unit of some kind. It's there, in the dark slick of the confinement that the screams are the most stuck in his head, a seven-inch that's been on repeat ever since you got home from the record store. He unfolds what's in his pockets, burning his knuckles on some broken shit from the heating unit, doesn't notice, slips the mask over his face. It's an old one, losing its thrill each day. But all he sees is purple, and it's quiet..

THE SKIN AND THE FLUID

Brown rainwater ebbs over the curb at the bus stop. The Director catches Vega before she gets on the bus, "I enjoyed your piece about Detective Castra."

Something floats by in the gutter, a brochure, maybe a rat.

"Thank you," Vega responds.

"It's the kind of story people come to this city for."

"Thank you. That was the goal, so that's great to hear."

"Well, what I really mean is that I enjoyed how you took Castra's violence and turned it into something marketable. It was beautiful in a way."

"She was a great interview. Easy to talk with," Vega shrugs with her mouth.

The bus closes its door, makes its way off down the street.

"Should you and I talk?"

"You want your story in the paper?"

"No, I want to give you a goddamn job, Vega. You've got some transferable skills that I want to see about. Plus, I need some demons."

The Director's apartment is moderately sized. The wallpaper lavish, bordering on macabre. She's in the kitchen, made smaller by the enormity of the cabinets, digging a small piece of machinery out from under a stack of concentric pots as Vega politely stares at the ceiling. With a quiet clattering, the Director places the machine, a small plastic tower with three tiered levels, a sharp silhouette against the sunset glowing against the window. The Director leans over, athletically, trying to get the plug into a warped power outlet. Until it clicks. The mechanism hums with a luxury that's unexpected from such thin plastic. Vega doesn't know the purpose of the machine until the Director empties an entire bottle of top-shelf wine into the bottom tray. A gurgling sound emerges, and then a different frequency of humming, thicker, slower, nearly strained. The wine spills itself out and pours from the top, dribbling its way down the tiered trays. A chocolate fountain oozing out Cabernet.

A glass plops in Vega's hand and they both fill their first drink. They talk, the detective learning that Vega's not from this city either and that people always swear that she's a local, ask her for directions in the most labyrinthine back doors of lounges and bars. But, Vega starts to notice what's happening, begins to ask her own questions, take her own control of the conversation. But it's only a wall from there. The Director shows her the mural painted across the bricks, but the kid isn't getting through this barrier. It's this resoluteness that begins to calm Vega, knowing where she can go and where she can't. Around the detective, the story is clear. The Director speaks of her travels. The items and curiosities, mementos, she's acquired along the way to fill her apartment like the storage room of a museum, items not old enough, or too plastic, to be artifact, locked up until time makes them worth enclosing in glass. Objects that have the shape of another era, before or after, but the material is there, right before you, cheaply present. She unrolls one of the objects in front of her, holds out the mat in front of Vega, invites her to run her fingers over the miniscule spikes.

"It's for blood flow. You've seen the acupuncturists, right? A few shops not far from the Disco you kids like to fuck around at. This mat does what they do in a way, nothing to stick around in your skin—despite the art of it—but it pains your mind into increasing circulation around each prick.

And, I want to say I once counted over a thousand of them. But, at the time I counted that I remembered counting something closer to seventeen hundred of them. But, I can forgive myself for miscounting needles."

Vega's losing trust in the conversation. It's on her face, coming loose at the eyes.

"The reason I'm showing you. Is that it'll help you sleep."

"I missed my bus for this."

"That's the job."

"Sleep?" Vega asks.

"Sleep. You're able to palate monstrous things. And that's what you're going to do. This is going to help you relax. The circulation. You've brought demons in before. Everyone has. This will be different though. We can talk rates after the first session."

"There are demons I don't want to see again."

"We can't choose the ones that come back," the Director's almost sad.

"I don't know what to do then."

"We'll talk rates after the first session," the Director counts out her words.

"It's not that."

"I'm not going to read your fucking mind, kid."

"I'll do it. But I don't like it," Vega shrinks into her shoulders.

"No one likes demons."

"I don't like that you know that I like demons. That I stay up at night just so I can fall asleep the next afternoon, bring one to the bedside. I've even gotten more than one. Up to three one Saturday. I'd stayed up all night and let myself fall asleep hard at noon–it's like all the sleep stored up breaks down some kind of wall. I woke up bricked down to my mattress and the three of them were wringing their hands over each other's heads and necks."

"When was the last time you slept?"

"It's… been a while," her face looking hollow, almost hungry.

"Lay down on this. The circulation will remedy that."

The Director lays the needled mat across her bed, then escorts herself to a corner of the room where she can perch her thin body on the arm of a heavily cushioned chair, a twisting pattern doing its best to writhe on out of the fabric.

"I'm just going to lay on it."

"Take off your shoes."

Vega leaves them on her feet. They're red pleather boots.

She climbs onto the mass of the bed, undoing itself with its unreal sized comforter, also patterned with dark tensile threads. Positions herself just in front of the mat, her back postured straight above it, parallel with the little spikes she can't see as she stares at the wall, refusing eye contact with the Director.

"This is supposed to hurt at first."

The Director responds as if she's said this before, "You don't have to explain it to me."

"It'll feel better once my body acclimates, once the needles are pushing into my skin for long enough."

"You've done this before."

"No," she lays back. "It just seems that way… I'm tired."

The mat is painful, a thousand little pains. The wine dribbles out of the fountain in the next room.

"Is it warm yet?"

"It's painful."

"That's normal."

"It's a bed of needles," Vega almost chants as she stares at the ceiling.

"I know—I'm just saying that it'll get warm, the circulation. That's when you can relax. But try to let loose before then. That'll help you sleep."

There's a few inches more of conversation between them, the distance between exchanges growing longer with each turn. And Vega, still staring at the gray of the ceiling, the sight and image of the Director pushed behind an obscuring corner in her mind, falls asleep.

First is a Pretty Face. Rattles a dresser from the inside, little by little, until the top drawer slides open by a hand's breadth. It begins crowning, birthing its head through the cramp of the drawer. Until there's an arm, a leg, the torso falling wet on the floor. It wanders to the bed, like it's the very same bed it leaves every night for a piss and a drink of water, able to walk back in the dark by muscle memory alone. It collapses onto the comforter. Rolling, slow. Drying off the liquid that stuck to its body in the moment of passing though. The fabric changes color by a shade with the new substance drenched into its woven threads. Finally dry, the demon scurries a little, only a few crawling movements, until it collapses again, an arm fallen across Vega's breathing stomach. Faceless, the demon imitates sleep.

The Director slings her feet out from underneath her ass–she'd gotten so comfortable–but she's never seen a demon show intimacy. Runs to the other room for another glass of wine. By the time she gets back, a Feather is arched over her with its hands on the headboard and its heels on the bed, rolling its head in a corkscrew motion, such a rotation that its feathers quiver with what looks like pain to the Director. The familiarity of a spinning head is nothing to her, but the slightest quiver of those feathers–it gets her every fucking time. She's sick in her neck, sick behind her own eyes. It's close to unbearable. She doesn't even notice the demon, a Pretty Face reaching over from the floor on the other side of the bed, stretching its limb across the sheets, wrapping unconscious fingers around the arched Feather's ankle. It begins to pull. It begins to get violent. A clawing, but then with soft fingers, rubbing the demon flesh until there's a thin, moist layer showing underneath the top skin. The Feather is crazed from Vega, not noticing, rotating its head further. The flesh begins to rub off in larger chunks now, the little Pretty Face seeming to get serious about its goal.

It's not much further, the Director guesses, before the limb is severed from the foot. She leaves the room again. Getting what she needs out of the kitchen pantry, she turns around to see three Pretty Faces reaching their mouthless heads under the flow of the wine falling from the fountain. They're thrilled, quivering with the idea of intoxication. Ignoring the sight, walking back in with a confidence forced only for herself, holding a broom in both hands, she steps over a formation of flesh–not sure how many demons are beneath her feet.

Shaking, only a little, she holds the broom above the bed, about to push the Pretty Face's clawing hand away. The demon, with the surety of a ritual, breaks the shaft of the broom. As if by instinct, it drives the stake in between where its eyes would be. The fluid inside its head slides thickly up the stake, streaming against gravity until it begins to run across the arched Feather's body. Wrapping, entwining. Gathering around a few scars that the Director hadn't noticed until now. She watches from behind her chair as the fluid seeps into the Feather's flesh, leaving no trace of a scar. A miracle, and she vomits bilious wine from the back of her mouth. Her chair changes colors by a few shades with the splatter of her nausea.

Two more demons rush in from the door, tending to the ankle wound, rubbing their face, squeezing their temples in stress with weeping movements. Another from the closet begins collecting the Director's vomit in the palm of its hands. It carries the light load to where it came from, coming back out of the closet with its glistening birth layer even thicker than before. Vega, untroubled and paralyzed, continues to sleep. A Feather wriggles too fast out from in between the cushions of the vomit chair and crashes to the floor, its head slinging with whiplash into a leg of the bed, cleaving the soft dome in half. The demons who'd just been tending to the ankle–having only made it worse, stripping the flesh further up the leg–descend on the split head.

They can't put it back together. Slapping the two sides together, wet meat, over and over with frustration, futility.

They beat their fists on the floor. It shakes the cloven head and they throw their own heads back and seem to convulsively weep. A whole cackle of demons arrives, this group entering from the cracks in the ceiling falling on each other. The distance is only eight feet, but they slap each other in an orgy of absolute pain. Something is happening where they're coming from. Bringing their own suffering onto this plane. A sleeping intern conjuring their writhing numbers.

For a moment, the Director glimpses the fountain of wine in her kitchen, catching a glimpse between the bodies. But, a demon's emerging from it too. The bitterness slicking it in a thin veil of burgundy. Furious, this one rails into the room, climbing over the flesh to get to no one particular demon. Searching among the number–the Director's lost track minutes ago–for not a single one. No body language of recognition. No conviction. Only searching. The bodies begin to open.

The burgundy one is splitting them, digging fingers deep, pulling with shaking effort, searching even more desperately, but the only things to find are more demons emerging from skin flaps, also searching. They're stacked on each other like a fever. The Director suffocates at a rapid rate. Vega. She's still asleep. The demons haven't touched the one in paralysis, the one who made the great split. He's crawling up on the headboard of the bed, crouching in rest. Because this is his best work so far.

From one of the splits–this one stretched across the leg of a Feather, the area that would be called the calf on a human body–a point squeezes itself, indulgently, out of the opening. It's sharp, like a sacrificial blade, something crafted for movement, dance, music, sex, glistening lights. It's a tooth. Made sharp by masochistic whispers running along their edges.

Other bodily openings contract around their own emerging teeth. They push themselves to a final height until they fall flat on the skin and the fluid. The layers of flesh start to convulse, turning the loose teeth, guiding them toward a center on the floor of the room. They inch toward each other, unassuming. And, when the sharp points touch, the sound is like a breeze coming from the ceiling. And as they wrap against each other in the center, they start to make a new noise, as they form into a shape, drawing loose flesh into themselves, forming a body after birth. It's the sound of a spine aligning, cracking satisfyingly into place.

A face made of only teeth, flesh so soft it seems edible to the air. An immaculate formation of a Whisper Teeth.

They're gone by the time she wakes up. Eyes closed for the whole thing. A dark, dark sleep. So rested she feels guilty. But she sits up too fast, the needles stubborn in her skin. Like another flesh weighing down on her own. That's when she sees the Director's body on the floor.

She did an experiment ten years ago. The teacher had laid out plastic containers on all of their desks by the time they'd arrived. It was the first time they'd all done their homework. One task. And it was to bring the bone of a chicken to school.

All of their nostrils burned when the teacher poured the vinegar. The air was one single acid by the time all the containers had been filled. But, this was the moment they'd been waiting for. On the count of three-two-one, they were to drop their chicken bone in the vinegar. Vega dropped hers on three. The little acidic bubbles were vibrating to the surface of the vinegar by the time everyone else let go of their bone. Weeks later, they peeled the lids off of each container and the acid was back, flatter this time, an opaque smell that was difficult to see through. Then, the little miracle. The chicken bones had been reduced to rubbery ghosts of their former brittle selves. Vega bent that bone, twisted it into new shapes, until it broke weeks later.

That was the state of the room she woke up in. The contortion of the Director on the floor. The walls, the bed, slick with something half-dried. The sheer act of consciousness burning her sinuses. Her fingernails chip away at a crust forming on her blankets. She emerges from the bed. Feet stuck to the ground in unfamiliar ways. Passes the corpse. Leaves the apartment. It's late in the hallway, nothing but dim lights and a couple–hardly aware that the other lover exists–keying open their door.

Vega explains only a little, the exasperation of her internship pressing down on her lungs–only a few proud words coming out. Something about why her clothes are oozed against her bones. That it's just been one of those shifts.

INTERLUDE – THE TOURISTS NEVER MAKE IT!

The tourists always come in, but they're the first to leave. It's probably the antagonistic arrangement of the shelves. Set up in a way that might lead some to believe there's a minotaur in the middle of it, reading pulp comics while he waits to tug at the skin of a human with his teeth. If the minotaur somehow gave birth, the damp little monster would have to work its way out in circles, first through the pulp it was born into, then mansion-imprisoned murder mysteries, past a more categorical shelf: local histories, ecologies, stolen courthouse records of family trees that have disappeared somewhere along the line, a single stack of books acquired secondhand from dropout med school students, an illustrated collection of extinct sea creatures, shelves of ax horror–all titles written by the same author, then an architectural honeycomb of rooms devoted solely to arcane symbols and the spells of languages that have been dead since their conception. The tourists never make it past this point. But, if they'd only muscle through, they would, in theory, see the wretched newborn beast, leaving hoofprints of afterbirth on the bohemian carpets. There's a carefully torn comic book panel, an action shot of the heroine leaping from the moon, stuck to his bloody forehead, like he's playing an esoteric game of Blind Man's Bluff. That's when the idea of the minotaur starts to break down. The further he journeys from the center of the bookstore, the more he grows into something entirely different. Clothing sprouts wretchedly from his skin. His legs narrow, pale, and lengthen. His horns fall to the floor like wet paper. He's a tourist now. He's wandering the shelves with his hands held gentleman-like behind his back. Nothing is for him. Nothing piques his human interest. And pretty soon it's time to leave.

GRIMOIRE RADIO - CALL #3

"Good evening, Murder City. That was Diana Ross. The seven tracks before her? That was Abba. You just can't get enough of those mother-fuckers, can you? To each their own, dear listeners.

I'm DJ Calling Card, taking your calls for Grimoire Radio, the segment where we segue from the music to your stories with none other than the city's sleep paralysis demons. We've got Pretty Face stories. We've got Feather stories. We're always eager for a Whisper Teeth story.

Darling caller, tell us your name. And tell us about your demon."

"Netti."

"That's one of those names that sounds familiar. Have we met?"

"No, I don't think we've met, DJ Calling Card."

"Maybe it's just one of those names. Like a song that's been stuck in your head, but you've never actually heard it before."

"Exactly like that."

"Well, Netti… Are you gonna tell us the story?"

"It's a Whisper Teeth."

"Sorry, for the pause there, Netti. I'm just not used to people actually phoning in with this experience. I'm… elated."

"It was a while ago. I only heard its words."

"Tell us what it said, Netti."

"That it saw a hooker. She was working in the hotel room with a guilty client. He kept talking about his family until she got so fucking sick of it that she took one of those ice buckets and caved his face in with it."

"Not an uncommon scene for a Murder City hotel."

"Yeah, I know that. But, the part I hated was how I could see it. And I'm used to that. Seeing the faces get eviscerated. That's just life here. But, it was my dad's face."

"God. There are no words, darling."

"He was a detective. Strong jaw. Fit the bill perfectly. So, when the bucket turned that all into mush… it was a lot."

"I don't mean to make light of this with a cliche, Netti, but, it sounds like you have some work to do."

"I do. Don't get me wrong, I do. But, it's not like that. Revenge. I just need… It's hard to say what I'm feeling. I just need to go further than I've gone before. To let myself go that far."

WOLFMAN RUNNING INTO THE WOODS

Netti and Castra kneel in the blood, exhausted. A thin sheet of guts runs from out of the club door and surrounds them on the sidewalk. She points a camera at the open split running across a body's stomach to its leg. The shutter clicks, pauses time between the two shitty detectives, and illuminates the edges of the wound's opening. She lowers the camera, squints at the gore. Raises her camera, but only to her chin, takes another shot with the flash.

She points, her fingernail so close it just barely touches a trickle of dark fluid, "See, you can tell this wasn't a slice job. Much more of a stab and saw. Tough to do with a moving target and a blade without serration. It's an entirely different kind of killer from the slicing type."

"God."

"It's not as bad as it sounds. The time from wound to death would have been short, roughly two minutes."

"Must have been a big two minutes."

"Some are bigger than others—you're not wrong."

"Did you see the DJ anywhere? In all of this," Netti circles his finger around the shapeless blood.

"Probably, what do they look like? I saw a few DJ types."

"Which types?"

"The type that doesn't deal in seven-inches," he holds up both hands in a way that could be a gesture for a record or a dick. "Only twelves so they smoke in the side rooms."

"Okay, that's fine."

"What are you thinking about?" Castra asks, examining a stretched out flesh sack on the concrete.

"Nothing, I was just trying to recreate the scene in my head. Would make more sense with music."

"You don't have to get defensive–you're allowed to ask questions."

"That's funny."

"What?" Castra asks, already knowing, obliging.

"It's just that on TV all the detectives are total cock blocks about who gets to ask the questions."

"I've never thought about myself as much of a cock block detective."

Netti stands up, balances a little in the puddle of guts, "Go on about that."

"At the end of the day, the detective's more of a priest than a cop. Not the priest on the other side of the screen in the confession box. More like the priest that shows you her tits at the human sacrifice. She leads you through the violence, guides you around the knife, makes some sense of it. No meaning without the priest, just some asshole with his throat cut. The city's lost without her. I mean, how do you think this city got so chest-fucked? No detectives. A bunch of corporate goons fulfilling their job descriptions. But, by the time the case is closed there's no blood on the idol and her eyes are nothing but granite–staring at a pile of fucking paper-work. Think about it, no more secret halls in the temple. Just office spaces getting flooded with overflowing ashtrays. And what are you supposed to do with that? Case files smudged out with cigarette ashes? Doesn't make a damn bit of sense. But that's where you need the priest. To make some kind of sense of the violence—for the city at least. Because, the priest sure as hell knows it doesn't do a damn thing for her. There is no sense. Just a bucket of blood spilled for a stone face someone said was god. But, to offer a reason behind the knife. Now, that's a fucking job. That's her job."

Netti, unsure, responds, "You're a good priest."

"I'm not the priest, Netti. Jesus. I'm here to shoot kids taking drugs. That's my job. You're the one who's the priest. The last detective at the altar. Don't fuck it up."

They're headed to the Disco for the last time. Netti, the Mixing Boys bouncing obediently toward the club, the whole marketing team filed behind Detective Castra in anticipation of her next story. The air around them is swollen, monolithic, creaking back and forth in the night before it bursts open. One of the Mixing Boys is rubbing a knot out of his own shoulder with one hand and arguing the place of vermouth amongst the classiest drinks of all time. Castra's describing the process of establishing time of death based on how swollen the body is and how to tell how long it's been at the bottom of the river.

The whole situation carries the taste of a bad memory–Steph's book club all over again.

It was highschool when everything had the aftertaste of pills. He'd been to the club several times before, and Steph continued to invite him back because he was already there to begin with. Every member carried pulverisingly heavy tomes into her room and they circled around, sitting under the outstretched drawers of a dresser, perched on top of the vanity, tucked under the cosmicly printed covers of her bed at absurd angles. He was simply sat on the floor, thumbing through a copy that the girl next to him let him read just a few minutes before the discussion started–high, but only off of a joint he bent up and dropped in a flower pot out back, using his fingertips to cover it in wet soil until there was no twist of smoke. There was a handful of pills in his wool coat pocket and he thought about it like a new parent thinks about sleep, begging the sun to bury itself in the earth.

The discussion began, but not before they did a synchronized knocking on the floor and furniture around them, three quick raps and too slow to signal the discourse would begin. One of the girls lying under the covers complained about the form. Intro, Argue, Counterargue, Prove, Conclude. The drudgery of it! But she was quick to explain how the pathos of it somehow shone through, that it transcends logic, or subverted, she wasn't sure which one. A girl, this one leaning against the dresser, argued against her. Another, with a middle path, inserted herself. Netti scooted himself across the floor until his back was pressed against the wall. His wrists hung over his knees, waiting for the sun to go down.

He was one of them, in the circle, but never a part of it.

Steph came in with her take, spelled out an extravagant metaphor teeming with ultraviolet energy. She framed it with her hand motions from time to time and everyone of them, but Netti, leaned forward to catch each dive of the case Steph was presenting. He couldn't hang. He slipped the first of his pills out of his pocket and into the back of his throat. The one under the dresser caught him, said nothing. After several more turns of conversation, he'd relocated to his side of the circle.

A warm whisper in his ear that he truly hates, "Can I have one of those?"

He's hesitant to share, unsure how it might make the discussion last even longer if these girls were feeling good.

He ignores her, at first, adding what he can to the discussion, "Sure, I liked the words, but mostly the illustrations. The cross-hatching was so thick it just looked blacked out. Heavy." Netti's voice is distant, self-conscious of the class-clowenery of his comment.

Steph chips in, "Netti, you can't just come to book club and talk about the picture you saw two minutes before we started discussing."

"It's not my fault the illustrations are the best part, Steph," he doubles down.

Steph brings it all back to the form of argument, how it functioned as a motif throughout the text. Netti responds by handing the girl to his right two or three pills. Throws back another for himself. It's only by the time that the discussion gets into the granular details of the second chapter that both of their pupils are constricted and they're seeing the discussion in a whole new way.

The form and the details begin to fade and pretty soon everyone's discussing the illustrations again, the heavy-lifting they do for the flow of the book. Netti even goes so far as to say the flow is unnecessary in light of the line work and he hands out a few more pills. One's organizing Steph's clothes in anticipation of the high. Another's dancing with her tongue shot out as she expects it to dissolve in effervescence in her saliva. Another one's waiting on their first pill to kick in, and Netti and the other already euphoric, completely unaware of the other, relishing in the descent of the rest of them. Except for Steph. She's on the floor, leaning back against her own bed, the book closed and weighing down her knees. And he's been wondering for goddamn years how many talking points she'd planned, how, if he wasn't there, they'd still be goddamn discussing. It could have been the city's greatest book club.

In the alleyway, Netti thinks about his sketches from the work day, how he couldn't really capture the motion of the wolf as he fell from his perch on the rafters into the middle of a seance. But, what he did capture, he assured himself, as the teeth-flashing of panic, that he was following a different plan now.

Tonight, there's a group of jumpsuits rearranging the sign above the Disco, looking over their shoulders from the ladder, hanging up black letters reading STUDIO 69 against the purple sunset. The Mixing Boys are slapping each other, like all of this had been building up to just a mild prank. Netti's face reads like someone who's seen a lamb get its arteries cut open.

Below the sign, the bouncers are motioning them inside. They'd been paid to look away for their prank and the five minutes was up. The boys link fists and make a small shelter of limbs over the marketing team, snapping their heads back and forth as if they're sneaking in a shipload of contraband. The bouncers are over it by the time they're vanishing behind the door. Detective Castra walks through them with an insufficient amount of bills but no one's counting tonight. Netti's having trouble keeping up, distracted by a group exiting the club, dressed like what has to be a new agency in town. He pauses to count on his fingers the number of frames he gave to the wolf's fall, then recounting how many more he would give him if he had to do it over again.

The club is writhing with smiles. Couples making out in the corners and on the floor and it almost sounds like their separate rows of teeth are clicking, pushing together. They don't notice the body in the mask cutting down dancers that have gone into a thin hallway leading to the breakroom. The haze of the employees' smoke break fills the claustrophobic space, and they're dead too. Blood wriggles out of bodies. The Killer stands at the far end of the hall in rest.

The bodies make a long, slender barrier between the Killer and the crowd. Nearest to the hall is a small group of dancers on more quaaludes than the others on the floor. They bend slowly, tightening their jawlines a millimeter every handful of minutes. Their knuckles, fingers, wrists tangle in with each other, indiscriminately. Their heads move in circles drooping downward toward the floor. One in their group begins to fall, ankles tangled with a complex step, but the others catch him in their arms and he can feel their muscles flexing steadily underneath his spastic body. They're not worthwhile to the rest of the floor – a relaxing pattern on the walls, an effect that doesn't make itself known. No one looks at them. No one sees the violence and the Killer standing still on the other side of them. All so fucking wicked. No one gets a break.

The DJ drops a slow jam on the table. A velvet baritone voice pushes down on the back of everyone's necks. Couples who've never met before tonight cling to each other for dear life—ecstasy or the dangers of the city tangling them up. Dangers just past their freshness, past when people spoke in empathetic tones in the checkout line saying I know, I know, never seen anything like it. The pain had settled in. Made bones out of itself. And so they shake their hairsprayed sculptures of hair together. Sweat dismantles updos and waves. Perms come undone. The drugs begin to edge and clusters of dancers make their way off the floor. The slow jam spins its way into an outro. Then, they reappear with new liveliness – like saints returning from the wilderness of cocktail tables and deep green bathroom stalls. Their kneecaps bang against one another and no one even winces. No one grits their teeth when stilettos sink into neighboring feet at pigeon-toed angles. There's even a glint of acrylic fingernails across eyelids, but any pain has retreated with the silence.

The Killer seems to be having a nice enough time, drifting the halls and backrooms. The mask over his face tonight—layers and layers of opaque tulle, bridalesque. Stitched into the material are a flock of reflective beads. The pattern seems to mimic the movement of something familiar, but not able to be placed. It's like the memory of learning a skill you can no longer perform, the rules of a game, the punchline of a joke, the order of the silverware set out on the table. The beads shimmer with the reflection of one man's particularly colorful shirt.

Beyond the dance floor are a series of booths, catching the sound in the purple of their faux leather cushions. Netti, having abandoned the ones he came with, stands between two groups, straddling the line between their booths. He shakes a teal drink in the direction of one group as speaks in the direction of the other. He's sweating under his fur coat and his face is soaked. He smiles, having been in this situation before. A waiter comes to the group he's speaking with. The pattern continues and his attention drifts over to the next table without even moving his feet at all. The pattern continues and by the third round of drinks-each one of his cocktails virgin-he's reaching out grabbing the hands and shoulders of his new friends as he gasps in disbelief about their shouted anecdotes.

"You know, I ran into the temptation when I was a student here at the community college. Are you from the area? Okay, so you don't know Barrion Technical College. I was just going to specify if you did, but the story makes sense without it. Anyways, when I was in school, I was taking this class on the clerical side of forensic work and basically how to bury your own body in a pile of waivers, and my professor didn't believe in grades, but she said they were a necessary evil. So she based our whole grade off of one project, and we could choose whatever we wanted to do for our project as long as it at least kinda had to do with forensics.

So I did my research on this time when the police couldn't tell if it was a coven of witches or just standard violence against neighbors going on in this one suburban town. Everyone was losing their minds because people were going missing and each missing case coincided with the mysterious appearance of a rune, or something like that, painted on the doorway of the person at hand. They all tended to be teenagers so a lot of people wrote this off as a fad, something the kids were doing. And one of the bizarre aspects of the case were some missing police officers. In a PSA, they tried to put people at ease by painting runes on their own door. They went on the evening news about it and assured everyone that they'd be conducting business as usual. But of course they started to disappear as well. The rest of the town turned into a roiling ball of moral panic.

People started reporting the runes were smudged against shop windows, or sidewalk chalked on the pavement. Even some people saying that they were built into the city-planning, that the roads formed runes when you looked at it from the top of the bookstore. But the thing was that a lot of roads are shaped like runes. It's just basic angles and shit. People really were disappearing though. Out of schools, hospital beds, neighborhood birthday parties.

The weird thing was that the runes were pretty much gone after a couple weeks, except for a few of the kids who were still fucking around. People still disappeared. And it went on for about a year, until these disappearances really just stopped. You could argue that the effect of the runes wore off after people slowly let them go or that it was something else entirely. Since then, they haven't found a single body, and nothing like it has happened since."

"Is that what happened here? Witches?"

"Oh no, it's not from witches. The story doesn't have to do with anything. Just interesting to see how people react to this sort of thing. Like you, you're a tourist. How wild is that!"

"Anything to see a demon," she laughs.

"Well, I'm sure you already know this. And it's probably why you're here in the first place. But it's pretty common to see them at the Disco."

He sighs, only just now seeing that the Feathers and the Pretty Faces are gathering at all the exits, coiling around each other in layers until every door is piled shut with demon bodies.

The circle of friends on quaaludes is next. They die in slow motion separate from their screams. The sound is in real time and the effect is paralyzing to the other dancers around. The Killer moves at no speed at all—not fast or slow, only something other than stillness. With a few more deaths on the floor, the blade begins to match pace with the music. It's perfect, choreographed. And in an awful way it seems like the music is following the movements of the blade, that the weapon is causing the beat itself, in the same way that the curved point is causing their bodies to open and bleed.

The Killer steps over the pile that was a slow circle moments before. The rest of the floor is thinning out. Crowds piling, clogging at the doors.

The DJ has her face buried in the mixing table. A 7-inch spins beside her head, catching and skipping like something sad and haunted, beating aberrant syllables into the walls around them. The bartender is pouring liquor into the wounds and mouths of several bleeding ones. Shards of glass lodged into her own arm but she hasn't seemed to notice. Netti and both of the groups he was speaking with have pushed their booths together and flipped over their tables to barricade themselves further from the crowd and the Killer.

The bodies inside their makeshift fortification are frothing over one another and Netti is wriggling his way to the top. He throws a fur coated arm over the edge and pulls his face up above it all. The Killer's not far off. His mask is beautiful.

He can't get over it. He's seen the masks of Pretty Faces made from woven twigs. He's seen coverings of feathers held together by globs of paint. Broken glass strung up with fishnet leggings. There was even one time when he pulled one apart piece by piece and he held up each chicken bone to the light, already bleached by the sun. Clean little needles had been driven through the bones—crudely, quickly, the points bent and broken—to hold the mask together. Something about having no facial features—these demons find it awfully fucking tragic. Desperate to shroud it with whatever pain they can find.

This mask is different, no shame in its construction. The veil-like fabric folds so intricately over itself it's like it's infinite in all its portions and divisions. The bead work is resolute, but still impossible to trace when it comes to searching for the pattern it forms so confidently. And the way it moves, each angle reveals something unseen about it as the Killer swings downward on the bodies of his victims.

There's a well-dressed boy in a blue corduroy jacket who's just been beheaded with five or six swings of the blade. Minutes later, someone will wade through the blood to fasten an ascot tourniquet around the gushing of his neck. It almost fits, but won't secure tight enough, no where close to stopping the heaving of blood. Keeps slipping off the edge of his neck, only to be redone uselessly with wet knuckles.

The DJ and the backup DJ are already dead; a woman in a sunset-colored jumper has taken over the turntables—hot, dead blood rising between her toes. It feels choreographed, the gore splatter across her face in time with the beat. It's a four-on-the-floor. The needle wallows in the vinyl groove. The head of the new DJ nods absently to the rhythm.

The sound system warbles, vibrating with the blood spray. The Killer's in a corner with his back pressed against where the walls meet. The intricate moulding of the walls is condensation with the sweat that's filled the atmosphere of the club. Dancers hold each other back from the blade, mash their foreheads together with tenderness and grit, shouting plans on how they're going to kill this motherfucker as he just waits in the corner, staring at the ceiling, his blade turning idly in a slender hand.

In pairs, the dancers charge the Killer, one swinging high and the other going for the knees. A man with angel wings pinned to his back pulls at the legs, gets cut straight down his spine. His partner in a fat leather belt almost has the Killer in a headlock, but gets de-limbed before doing any damage. It's the same pattern with the others. The pair in different shades of off-white. The double date with a fifth wheel in sequins and satin. Arteries gently opened with a body-sweeping movement of the blade. Vertebrae exposed to the color-changing lights. Segments of the bodies fall to the floor in wild, never-before-seen combinations. The Killer is a dancing wonder. He moves his body with elegance, his essence maintaining a complete void of effort or intention.

The numbers increase, dancers moving in mobs all at once, swallowing the Killer in writhing masses of flexed bodies. Each individual sinks into another, the pile lowering to the ground. The sound of the beat dampens against their varying layers of jackets, leather, costumes, and skin. The new dancers to the pile can hear the music diminish as they press their cheekbones into the body heat. The pile grows amorphously, until it stops, reaching a critical mass according to undiscovered rules written in the air. The chorus hits and all the club-goers have stopped to observe the work of their peers. That's when Netti falls into the still space on the floor dotted with the useless lights of a club in the throes of murder.

Netti looks around, finds a woman who most reminds him of Steph—it's the curly hair—and waves for her to come over to him. He points to the pile of bodies, "Did they get him?"

"Buried him, must be smothered. I feel for the folks at the bottom of the pile too. Surely, they're gone too."

Netti, knowing she'll die tonight, kisses her on the shoulder and walks away. Toward the doors.

It's getting strange now.

Feathers and Pretty Faces convulse over each other. He's never seen so many and, for a moment, wonders where they must have come from. One eats the one next to it, absorbing the other in violence, a sort of osmosis through the face. A kicking and screaming as it sinks into where there should be jaws on the face of a demon. All this through countless squares, so neatly dividing the violence beneath him. Netti feels his own throat slurping in the air, thick as honey with blood. A Feather brings a Pretty Face to the ground by its waist, begins the consumption by taking in a twisted-back arm. A Pretty Face rides the shoulders of a Feather, strangling its neck with bony knees—arms flailing victoriously, lifelessly above its head. And in the middle of all the hellish consumption is a single mask. He's dragging the blade behind him on the floor as he walks.

Gets pulverized to the floor, careless as to where the blade falls when he's knocked down. He's buried, appears in a different heap of bodies elsewhere in the fray, surgically cutting his way out of the stack.

His mask is unchanged. No frills torn. No shades darkened. The tulle is as lovely a veil as it was before the carnage. Thrilled, proud, he tilts his head to the ceiling. Drops his blade, finally, to the floor. Moving in his own trajectory, the plot of somewhere else dictating his movements.

All at once, with equal excitement, a face comprised of curved teeth erupts through the mask. Shreds the veil, tatters of it gliding back and forth as they fall to the floor, taking on the color of the disco lights. A Whisper Teeth all along. Wrapping its fangs around itself in an embrace of everything he's always been on this plane.

Netti's vomiting. Years of panic, nights spent rolling in bed thinking of cocaine, guilt that's beaten in his chest so long it calcified into an obstructive organ. Shitty dreams of being a detective. And, this whole time, there was nothing to make sense of. Just a demon in a mask, like the other demons in masks. Castra–she wouldn't have cared one way or another. Would have made a speech about it nonetheless. There's nothing left in his stomach, but he keeps heaving. Stumbling, trying to step out of it. Outrun the acid inside him.

The worst part is that he's known all along. Deep inside him, there was something prompting him to steal those demon masks. To wear them. As if wearing masks would help him unmask a killer. Between dry-heaving and catching his breath, he wonders if it worked, or not at all, and how he needed to leave this city either fucking way.

Until, in the middle of the dance floor, with no circle of dancers around it, is the demon's blade. It waits heavily on the light up tiles, iridescent green against the purple shades. It takes Netti a mile to get to it. As it waits between his feet, the head of a Feather falls to the ground.

A meandering trail of feathers tracks the plane of motion that the severed head followed. There's a growling hollowness between Netti's eyes and he simply has to fill it up.

The newborn demon is eating his way into the Disco. Still soaked from its emergence from Vega's sleep, it's closing its teeth around the demon bodies at the door. Jawing its way through the heave of limbs. Enough violence to cause the unmasked Whisper Teeth to turn its face. To feel what seems to be a kind of kin to itself.

It's only a few bounds and they're together. The masked one, running hands over the freshly arrived demon, scraping the fluid away by the palmful, first with its hands, then, gently with its teeth.

And by the time the new demon is dry, they've fully embraced. Barely discernible from the other. When they begin to consume, their bites eat up each other's skin as well as their own, indiscriminately. With equal ardor. Delicious, objectless lacerations.

A roiling pulp of skin and teeth. Its back is joyous, convulsing with the pure feeling. Netti runs the blade down the center of their single back. A neat gush of feathers and dust motes swell out of the slice in the skin. Testing, Netti digs the point down further. Dry vertebrae spill out; the point of a rib emerges from the gap. He shaves a little from the bone as the demon convulses, from pleasure, not from pain, his face digging deeper past the scalps into bones and gray matter. Netti wriggles the blade. The gap widens. It's dark and vacuous like the space past the edges of a memory, inviting, a presentation of the void.

He's not sure at first. But, he thinks he can see them. He needs a wider space to be sure, so he sinks his fingertips, at first, into the opening of the skin. Pulling outward. When little progress happens, he sinks his hands further up to the fur of his coat and he strains his arms. The feathers are damp between his fingers as the gap widens. The void becomes more clear, and that's when he's sure he can see the dreams of the demon.

They're decadent. Looking in, Netti tastes every question the Whisper Teeth has asked, but not of him. Do you mind if I try it with you? Have you ever felt the space between lung and bone? Deeper than you'd think, but you'd like to try wouldn't you? You know that was me who tried with you, right?

With a quick turn of the demon's body, Netti faces the Teeth. Its fangs undulating. The skin at the top of its maw, taught. Tender. Gristled around the edges. He thinks of the time he could have told Steph beforehand that he was a sleepwalker, perpetually placing the wrong guilts on the wrong objects. All the impossible, deathless guilts.

In the void of the demon's split-open back is the demon itself. It's chasing an intern as she enters the coffee shop, getting out of Netti's sight as quick as it can.

Inside the shop, it's counting the dust particles on the bottom of her shoe as she orders something hot at the counter. Kneeling, tracing a slight-angled symbol in the dust, invisible to her and unfelt. It leaves out the back and gathers a cloud of cigarette smoke from a barista, who only knows how to make a handful of drinks, on break. It presses the smoke into its teeth like the sweater of a lover lost. The river's nearby, only just on the other side of a small street used by three-wheeled trucks shuttling crates of brown-water fish to the restaurant chains to slice into filets and cover in bright sauces; waiters bring the dish out to guests, watch closely as they fork off the scales, saying oh my, it's busier than I expected.

The demon's waiting by the river, sharpening its teeth on a gum-molded curb, listening to the metallic clinking of dining all the way down the water. It's groaning from the throat at the pleasure of it, but not so loud that Netti can hear it back through the void from the Disco. This high is a good one, one of the best the Teeth's ever had. Newly jagged from the concrete, the demon's teeth tingle in the humid air. It's going to find some sleepers.

In an apartment complex across the river, it finds a trembling witch thumbing a thick line of blood across her headboard before going to bed. On her window sill, a tangle of flies is dying at a low volume. The witch sinks into her pillow and her left hand stains her comforter with the blood. The Teeth waits, sitting on the bedside table until it's allowed to consume the equivalent of her stomach.

Only one floor up is another witch. He's watching the cartoon about the wolf detective. He's burning through a joint with his eyes locked on the screen. The detective examines a table lined with Molotov Cocktails. Pulls out an impossibly long night stick from his coat pocket. Taps the glass of each one, so gently it's painful. His squinted yellow eye peering down the stick, both ears pointed through his hat like box cutters. He's testing to see which one will blow up in an act of future terrorism. Next, his magnifying glass swells the colors past the point of recognition. The Whisper Teeth loves this episode.

Now that the witch is asleep on the couch, it can caress his jaw with its teeth. He's cleanly shaven, which is a carnal disappointment. The sound of whiskers lopping off the skin is the closest thing to taking feathers as it gets. It tries to recreate with light cutting, but the effect just isn't landing. It sinks its teeth a little deeper and just removes his jaw. The breaking sound of a thick fruit.

Just one more stop before he goes back to the Disco for the Inbetweener.

He's in the break room at the agency. Rubbing his teeth against the heat of a coffee pot. Glorious, throat-tightening heat. The interns are making out in the intern office, more slowly than usual. And the Vest is flipping through the screen-printed boards of a campaign pitch for a lithograph company on its last legs. Unseen, it circles the room, traces its fingers through an ash tray, paws at the billowing shirt of the Vest. Then, it finds the notepad. Shaking just a little, it runs its palm over the thinly capitalized block letters. Then another page. And another page, shaking a little more this time. Human symbols fill it with wonder, the mystery never going deeper than its ink, forcing the meaning horizontally, infinite as long as it's perceived from a flat plane. It's pretty close to the end of the notebook when the Vest notices the signs of haunting. The magic is gone, and Teeth opens its jaws.

Back at the Disco, Netti hears an erupting of skin and bones. He looks up from the hole in the Whisper Teeth's back. Not far in front of him on the dance floor, he sees the Vest split from his stomach and fold to the floor. The Whisper Teeth, the one from its dreams, emerges from the gore like a newborn bull. Netti looks down at the Whisper Teeth in front of him, the same one that's on the floor sliding out of the Vest. There's a wet one, and a split one. The same one. But the wet one's coming over, crazed with the grinding of its teeth. Netti steps back from the split one.

The wet one glistens with its purple joy, pressing its teeth into itself, the split one. The teeth move slow, running through, emerging out of both sides of the body. Then it shakes, flinging feathers and skin chunks into the alternating-colored air. The satisfying sounds of ripping skin. Low growls. Clacks of teeth, rows of them. Netti looks away, quickly counts the pieces of the Vest, notices Detective Castra leaning against the wall with her hand on her gun, the Mixing Boys carrying drinks to the rest of the marketing team and stretching their arms around their young shoulders in consolation of their fallen Vest.

Eyes on the floor, Castra crouches down. Peers through the tangle of legs, sees flashes of teeth and bits of scalp fall to the purple tiles. Then the rest of several heads, shapeless gore held together only by a few flesh strands–some recognizable as tattered cheeks, torn and stretched eyelids. The crumbs of what's been eaten, fallen as the Whisper Teeth eats itself. A violence so dazzlingly brazen that it could swallow up all other violences in its proximity. A gravity unto itself.

Castra thinks: No more evidence. No more interrogations. No more using civilians to get closer to the assholes with drugs.

The Mixing Boys are hugging each other, rubbing the shoulders of the marketing team, handing each other drinks, hunching their shoulders away from the Whisper Teeth. Easy targets. But with a .32 snub nose, not all of the bodies would be the intended targets. The marketing team, fragments of them, at least, would go down too. Less of them than the Mixing Boys. Enough of them. But, it's the right price. A worthy counterargument.

She walks closer, feet barely off the ground like she's sloshing through a gutter. Picking up the pace. Running. Running like she's going to help, lead them to an exit that's not blocked by demon flesh. But, it's the barrel of her gun that's in the neck of a Mixing Boy. Fires upward. A step back, and she fires again. Another step back, more shots. Then an intern, the first accident. Then another, this one with intention.

They could try to stop her, but she's always one step back, releasing a bullet into an open screaming mouth. The heads of the Mixing Boys blend with the torsos of the marketing team. One more shot. One more Mixing Boy and it's over. But, the demon's self-meal is interrupted. A last step back from Castra and the fangs, gently, slowly, close around her arm. Supernatural accuracy, the way its teeth press down precisely on her arteries.

Little divots in the skin, at first, testing. Little squirts of blood, building in steadiness. Castra's known this would happen, for a long time—it's sloshed across her face. Her body twisted, folded onto itself in gentle breaking movements. The Whisper Teeth guides the contortion with over-eager limbs and surgically careful fangs. Directing all the blood, with all its momentum, to the right throbbing areas of the body. And then. One enormous sinking of the teeth. Black blood geysers to the ceiling, tinting the lights, streaming across the disco ball.

With the detective dead. The Mixing Boys, the marketers slaughtered. The demon bodies in a pile. Netti kneels in the slough and grabs a handful of black slicked feathers. There's some kind of feeling in the bottom of his Halloween scars that this is what he's supposed to be doing, that he's supposed to do, to be throwing at the back of his throat.

He wonders why, until he looks to the DJ table. And there she is, lit up in purple. And then it's black. The purple returns and she's a few steps closer to Netti. What he couldn't see before is that her stomach is streaked with fading green paint.

Another blackout of the lights and she's standing face-to-face with him when they streak purple again.

Frankenstein speaks, "The city wants to eat, Netti. That's why it opened itself up, to catch anything that might fall in. You fell in… But, this time isn't like that. The feathers—for ones like you and me—they aren't drugs, nothing like that actually. I'd say that we're immune to the effects, but that's not quite it either. See, it's less like a line of coke. More like sinking your teeth into yourself. Are you immune to yourself, Netti?"

He can see scars on her neck where plastic bolts would have been years ago.

Frankenstein continues, "You become your own city with your own pair of jaws. A new suit of skin. This whole time, I could see you in the skin already. And you look fucking beautiful."

He plans on savoring this hit. It's all quieting down. No fucking in the bathroom, no hackling from across the bar. The lights illuminate an empty bench and black out. A cocktail table with a hand in early throes of rigor mortis and black out. The disco ball weeping blood splatter and black out.

He tosses back the feathers.

Her footsteps drift further from Netti, but he doesn't watch as she walks away. Compelled by another plane, another plot, he's throwing his coat off his shoulders and sliding the sleeves off his arms. Skinnier than anyone would have known, eager to move without the weight of fur. Then he starts to look.

His insides feel like cheap candy, tired—bright. They're still sinking at the sight of his friend's bleeding arm, excited by the shade of blood. Throbbing that the asshole in the doctor costume took his new friend away. His guilt and anger doppelgänger him through those nights as he simultaneously suffers through this one, sifting through the gore, looking.

It's difficult to find in the layers of flesh on the dance floor, the slow-strobing lights illuminating the new configurations of bone and hacked tissue. He splays his fingers, runs them through the gore, feeling for the Teeth skin. The feel is impossible to forget, fittingly taut, slick like gums. It's in a moment of darkness that he hooks it with his thumb, slides it out from underneath someone's stiff dead face.

He holds the Teeth skin out for size. A perfect fit, slides his arms into the flesh like the world's first land creature returning to sea. He spins but it doesn't twirl with him, clasps itself close to his own skin. His movements feel damp, only slightly slower than before. The darkness. Only the sound of his own steps walking toward the door, now open as the demons have been eaten away.

He tosses the feathers at the back of his mouth. They spread across his teeth and cling to the back corners of his gums. Then, they regel as one mass, excited by the mix of fluids–except for one, clinging in between two of his molars. He swallows the mass of feathers but the one. He looks to Frankenstein but she's still not there.

Ceiling lights flicker toward their death. No high, no cocaine. It's the sweat of a fur coat.

Something inside his stomach, something that strings his stomach to his skin, pulls them a little closer together.

A shock of purple illuminates the street outside. Silhouettes pass by the open door–the ones who've made him hate being conscious, some of them with swords, others riding demons like pigs. He thinks of a Barry White lyric. The baritone. The beat. The extended seven-minute club cut. All the sweat that had soaked into his fur coat through the years. And then it happens.

The emptiness of the dance floor swells around him. Collagulates around his body. All that makes up nothingness in that moment presses into him. In his chest, he knows what's about to happen, thumbs the feather stuck between his teeth with his tongue. He crouches down as the demon skin begins to sink further into him. Erasing his own skin until it's somewhere else. Then his bones. And an organ, then another. The feathers simmering in the sack of fluid that was a stomach only just before he began to disappear.

He opens his eyes to more purple. But, by the time Netti realizes he's soaking wet, the space dims its color into the dark. The air's dense, thick around him, the sense of years that faded there. The fluid covering Netti is also anchoring his feet to the carpet. While he can't see, he reaches around for something to stabilize him. Banging his wrist against a ceramic pot, flinches and hits another one. He grabs on with both hands, steadying himself.

Fluids gleam across his face—can nearly see it in the dark. Stable. Breathing. Feeling the feather between his teeth with his tongue. It's dead now, no more wriggles. Netti thinks about how it must not have survived the journey. The spine of it is sharp and he tastes a little of his own blood.

No high. Not like he would have expected. Just numbness. Only the taste of bagels, sweat, the rubber of a wolf mask.

At the back of his throat, he stifles a laugh. Swallows down the laugh. And the gray shapes around him turn to purple for a moment.

Back to gray.

He's forgotten he's wearing demon teeth over his face. Looking at the light through a veil of fangs. He raises his hands to part the teeth away from his face. A few silent cuts in the process. The warmth of blood runs quietly from his palms.

His eyes are adjusting and the shapes show themselves to be a number of house plants. They smell like iron.

He's drying off slowly, unsure of how much time is passing. The toe of his shoe rising slightly from the floor, the fluid having condensed into something more solid, breaking lightly as he pulls his foot upward from the carpet. He takes a deep breath, and now that the smell of the fiber has settled back into his brain, he can begin to trace something else. He steps away from the wall.

And there he is. The foot of Steph's bed. It's the same room, the same dresser, the same comforter, the plants have aged beautifully—filling half the space with greenery thick enough to cut and flood the room with fluids that are fucking hungry for the sun. The shelf, warped slightly from the old weight of book club reads, is empty.

New, small plants have grown in their absence, the smell of a tangled jungle. Netti's wearing demon skin. And Steph's paralyzed with her head sunk into the pillow. But, he's not paralyzed in the way Netti would have guessed. The Steph he knew would have prided herself on how he was correctly paralyzed, arms, neck, teeth all where they're supposed to rest. But, this Steph is different. You can see it in her eyes, waiting as they lock with the ceiling. Netti thinks she knows.

The TV that used to show them scary movies, the cheap, shitty ones. Because it was a cheap, shitty TV. The pentagram carved into its faux wood side still just as scratchy as when they were kids. Netti's stifling another laugh, trying not to wake her in case Steph really is unconscious. This whole thing. So damn funny.

His demon skin has his body at a perfect temperature. It breathes. He's even a little cold.

He thinks Steph knows he's there. No real way to know.

But, he'll wait. He'll wait until morning, when his old friend will begin to cough and loosen her body and sit up and ask—Netti, my god, what happened to your coat?

But, before all that, he lays down beside her, on top of the blanket, his side pressed up to hers. Head on her chest, the blood of the demon staining her loose t-shirt. He thinks of this one movie they really loved, more than all the others they saw on lonely Saturday nights. Each other, the only bastion against crushing solitude.

There was this movie that came on probably once a month in the middle of the night, a werewolf flick. Netti thinks, realizes that the networks must have lined up the schedule with the lunar calendar.

The opening sequence was a long rain of names and titles darkening the full moon. And then it panned down to a back full of loose bones, plastic knobs under a sheet of latex, arranging and rearranging until they resemble a more lycanthropic spine, sprouting tufts of fur through the surface, bristling with a cheap howl running through the busted TV speaker. The camera pans back—nauseating speed. And then it's just a wolfman running into the woods. But Netti doesn't remember whether or not he gets shot between the jaws with a silver bullet.

He'll ask Steph in the morning, when she'll begin to cough and loosen her body and sit up and say—Netti, my god, I love your new coat!

ABOUT THE AUTHOR

Caleb Bethea is a writer from the Southeast. You can find their work in HAD, X-R-A-Y, Maudlin House, hex, Tenebrous Press, and elsewhere. But, mostly, they're just a family ghoul with a wife and four goblins by the ocean. Share your favorite disco track with them at CalebBethea.com